Everything was closing in on her...

Suddenly something inside her snapped, and the fear moved aside, making way for the anger. In the past two weeks she had been evicted from her home by the IRS, threatened by a commando fighter on the lam and interrogated by two Interpol agents. Now she was being victimized by a viciously cruel insurance investigator.

The scream burst forth from her throat and caught the man by surprise. He stumbled backward, his gun waving frantically. A gunshot splintered the air, and the door crashed open. Another shot exploded.

Bettina screamed until she thought the sound would echo in her head forever....

ABOUT THE AUTHOR

Andrea Davidson lives in Houston with her husband and two children. She began her writing career with the American Medical Association in Chicago. Since then she has written several Harlequin American Romances. The idea for *A Siren's Lure* came to her in a dream, but Andrea held off writing the book until she went to Capri with her husband and discovered the perfect setting for the story.

Books by Andrea Davidson

HARLEQUIN INTRIGUE
25–A SIREN'S LURE

HARLEQUIN AMERICAN ROMANCE
 1–THE GOLDEN CAGE
16–MUSIC IN THE NIGHT
21–UNTAMED POSSESSION
45–TREASURES OF THE HEART

These books may be available at your local bookseller.

Don't miss any of our special offers. Write to us at the following address for information on our newest releases.

Harlequin Reader Service
P.O. Box 52040, Phoenix, AZ 85072-2040
Canadian address: P.O. Box 2800, Postal Station A,
5170 Yonge St., Willowdale, Ont. M2N 6J3

A SIREN'S LURE
ANDREA DAVIDSON

Harlequin Books

TORONTO • NEW YORK • LONDON
AMSTERDAM • PARIS • SYDNEY • HAMBURG
STOCKHOLM • ATHENS • TOKYO • MILAN

For Jim—
who shared the experience.

───────────────

"Draw near," they sang, "illustrious Odysseus, flower of Achaean chivalry, and bring your ship to rest so that you may hear our voices. No seaman ever sailed his black ship past this spot without listening to the sweet tones that flow from our lips, and none that listened has not been delighted and gone on a wiser man."

Sirens' song from *The Odyssey*, Book XII, by Homer

Harlequin Intrigue edition published September 1985

ISBN 0-373-22025-1

Copyright © 1985 Susan L. Lowe. All rights reserved.
Philippine copyright 1985. Australian copyright 1985.
Except for use in any review, the reproduction or utilization of this work in whole or in part in any form by any electronic, mechanical or other means, now known or hereafter invented, including xerography, photocopying and recording, or in any information storage or retrieval system, is forbidden without the permission of the publisher, Harlequin Enterprises Limited, 225 Duncan Mill Road, Don Mills, Ontario Canada M3B 3K9, or Harlequin Books, P.O. Box 958, North Sydney, Australia 2060.

All the characters in this book have no existence outside the imagination of the author and have no relation whatsoever to anyone bearing the same name or names. They are not even distantly inspired by any individual known or unknown to the author, and all incidents are pure inventions.

The Harlequin trademark, consisting of the words HARLEQUIN INTRIGUE, with or without the portrayal of a Harlequin, are trademarks of Harlequin Enterprises Limited; the portrayal of a Harlequin is registered in the United States Patent and Trademark Office and in the Canada Trade Marks Office.

Printed in Canada

Chapter One

He was being led to the wall. He could not see the pale pink stucco surface gouged and pitted with bullet holes and scratched with the haphazard scrawlings of pro-government slogans. He could not see because of the blindfold that covered his eyes. But he knew it was there in front of him. He could smell it. And almost taste it. His every sense told him it was there.

He also knew that within minutes, maybe even seconds, the bullets that riddled his body would add more notches to the wall.

His hands were bound behind his back with his torn shirt, but they were tied loosely, and in another time and place he might have been able to get away. But not here. Not with these trigger-happy, prepubescent soldiers who were waiting impatiently to prove their manhood at his expense. For them, it was a rite of passage. For Erickson, it was the end of the line.

The hands on his arms turned him around, and he felt the cold wall against the bare skin of his back. A trickle of sweat fell from his brow, down his chin and onto his chest. Another followed.

6   *A Siren's Lure*

Suddenly, out of the hot darkness, a tremendous roar reverberated in his ears. It was a sound he had never heard before—the sound of his own death.

He bolted up in bed. The sheet below him was drenched with sweat. His heart was pounding. His breath was ragged and quick against the darkened night. Fear coiled like a tight spring inside him. He tried to focus on something real and tangible—the chair across the room, the dresser, the open bedroom door—anything.

He swung his legs over the side of the bed and fumbled for the pack of cigarettes on the table. Several fell to the floor, but he grabbed one in midair and stuck it between his lips. His shaky fingers searched the dark for the lighter, found it and lighted the tip of the cigarette. He stood up, took in a deep, steadying breath and walked across the room. The window was bare to the sky and the cliffs and the sea, the Faraglioni to the south, the coast of Sorrento and Amalfi just beyond view to the east. A full, cold moon hung over the island.

He stood there for a long time, smoking and staring out the window, letting the dream slip back into the past, where it belonged.

IT WAS A NIGHTMARE. The Aubusson tapestry, rolled up and tossed over a broad shoulder, was the next thing to go. Bettina Bacheller, standing in the middle of her almost bare living room, its red walls garish without stylish furnishings to temper the color, was helpless to stop what was happening. Nevertheless, she gave it a damn good shot.

A Siren's Lure

"You can't take that!" She hurled herself in front of the door, where another man was now trying to depart with the Berthe Morisot. *Young Woman in a Party Dress.* Her father's favorite. Her favorite. He had always said the painting resembled her. She didn't really think so, but because he had, she loved it.

"I'm sorry, miss," the man said, trying to edge around the beautiful but obstinate young woman in the doorway. "You've been served the Notice of Federal Tax Lien, then the Notice of Levy, then the Final Demand."

"But I've appealed everything! For many years, in fact!"

"Your appeals have been denied. You should have paid the taxes."

"I don't owe the taxes! This had to do with my father. It has nothing to do with me!"

"You now have the Notice of Seizure, ma'am. I'm sorry, but you'll have to step aside."

"Listen, I've had it up to here with all this legal rigmarole. Just who signed your orders to come here today?"

"Our orders come directly from Lawrence Harper."

"I'd like to know who the hell he thinks he is."

"United States Department of Treasury, ma'am. Commissioner of the Internal Revenue Service."

Bettina's glare didn't faze the man trying to get through the doorway. "I'm aware of his title," she spat. "Now, I'd like for you to get him on the phone."

"Sorry, lady, but my hands are full right now. You'll have to get him yourself and, ah, do you think you could move a little to the left? Thanks."

8 *A Siren's Lure*

With one final scowl, Bettina stepped aside and sagged against the wall. *Young Woman in a Party Dress*, gone. Everything was gone, or at least would be by the time these government agents were finished with her house. Her house. Her things. This wasn't happening. Not to her. Moments like this didn't happen in the life of Bettina Elizabeth Bacheller. Strange people couldn't just walk in and take control of all her possessions, could they?

She walked to the phone in the foyer, praying they hadn't disconnected that along with the rest of her life. "I need the number for the Internal Revenue Service," she said to the information operator. "The commissioner's office." She wrote down the number, redialed and waited for an answer.

"Lawrence Harper, please." She waited again for transfer to his office.

"Lawrence Harper, please." She was rapidly wearing thin on the pleases, but she said them anyway. She wasn't always polite—only when she thought it might help her get her way.

"May I give him your name, please?"

"No, you may not give him my name. It's the only thing I have left. But you may tell him Bettina Bacheller is calling."

"Is he expecting your call?"

"I have no idea if he's expecting my call or not." Her fingernails began to drum against the now bare wall.

"What is this regarding?"

"It is regarding the fact that half a dozen men are at this moment traipsing through my house, appar-

A Siren's Lure 9

ently under Mr. Harper's orders, and are carting off everything I own. That's what it is regarding."

"One moment, please."

God, when was she going to wake up from this nightmare! Maybe it was something she had eaten. She had drunk too much champagne last night. And it had been one of those domestic brands. That had to be it. Soon it would be morning, and everything would be all right. Her home and her life would be hers once more.

"I'm sorry, but the Criminal Investigation Department and the Collection Department are handling your case. If I could have your number, a special agent will call—"

"My number is in the book," Bettina growled. "And you can tell Mr. Harper that this little joke has gone far enough. I will not stand for this. I have lots of friends in the government and—hello...hello?"

She slammed down the phone, and the two men maneuvering the grand piano onto the dolly looked over at her. She turned her back on them, trying to ignore their all-knowing stares. She knew exactly what they were thinking. They had seen it all before: another deadbeat who was getting her just deserts.

She picked up the notice from the credenza and read it for at least the tenth time. Form 668-B of the Department of the Treasury—Internal Revenue Service. "The amounts shown above are now due, owing and unpaid to the United States from the above taxpayer for internal revenue taxes." She scanned through all the legal mumbo jumbo, getting to the crux of the issue. "So much of the property or rights to property as

10 *A Siren's Lure*

may be necessary to pay the unpaid balance of assessment shown are levied with the power of distraint and seizure by any means.''

Bettina read it again. *Seizure by any means.* In plain English, that meant only one thing—what was hers was now theirs.

She sat down in the only chair that had not yet been seized and closed her eyes. When had everything gone wrong? Memories of her childhood came back to her in fragments. The most vivid were those of traveling with her father. Although he had traveled extensively, she was thirteen before he had taken her on her first trip. They had gone to Egypt and been treated like royalty everywhere. Nothing had ever been too good for Stephen Bacheller's little princess.

She didn't remember her mother—other than a few peripheral impressions—although Bettina had seen the photographs of her before she became ill. She had died when Bettina was two, and it had been only father and daughter—Stephen and Bettina Bacheller—ever since she could remember. Of course, they had always had a series of live-in help, caretakers to watch over her while her father was away on business. But those people never counted much in her life. They came and went without any fanfare and did not leave any lasting impressions on her. Stephen was her family. She had known, in her child's heart, that it would be just the two of them forever.

And it had been. Almost. Oh, she had gone away to that art school in Geneva and to Mount Holyoke for college. But they had spent lots of time together, traveling, entertaining and being entertained, or just sit-

A Siren's Lure 11

ting quietly in his study and making grandiose plans for their future.

She opened her eyes and looked up at the two men standing over her, waiting to take the chair she was sitting on. The fantasy world of Bettina's childhood had ended. That security and prosperity had lasted for twenty-eight years. Now, reality had finally reached her doorstep. The real world of Bettina Bacheller was that the government of the United States had taken over her house and possessions and had branded the father she had adored a criminal.

She stood up and, in a daze, walked through the foyer, out the front door and down the sidewalk to her car. All her suitcases and as many boxes as she could pack of things exempt from the levy filled the backseat and trunk of her Mercedes. She watched the government agents stretch a chain across the front door of her town house. From the chain hung a metal sign that claimed the house as the property of the United States government. Soon it would go up for public auction.

Back taxes and penalties. Everything she had inherited from her father was now reduced to that.

Chapter Two

Bettina was on her first vodka martini. He was on his second glass of scotch.

"I don't believe it, Jerry. Not for a minute. And I know you don't either." She kept her green eyes riveted on his face. "Do you?"

Jerry McCluskey was unusually somber that evening. He was always a quiet, thoughtful sort, but around Bettina it was generally impossible for him not to be affected by her spark. Not tonight—not when he had this kind of news to discuss with her. This was not the time or the place for sparks. He watched her hands instead of her eyes. She was fingering her glass, stirring the ice with the swizzle stick and wiping off droplets of condensation from the outside.

"Well, do you, Jerry?"

"Bettina," he said to her smooth, manicured hands, "they have a...an overwhelming amount of evidence to support this case."

She tossed her head, and her long, blond hair flipped back over her shoulders. "Evidence! Oh, I see. It's guilty until proven innocent; is that it?"

"Okay, 'proof,' if you like that word better."

A Siren's Lure 13

"Proof. Proof that my father is some sort of...of international jewel thief. That is really the most outrageous nonsense!"

Jerry fingered his short beard and glanced across the room. The jazz pianist had switched pieces and was now playing a Gershwin medley. *An American in Paris* was the first number. Jerry looked back at Bettina. "He was almost caught in France, you know."

She vigorously stirred the ice in her glass.

"I know it must be hard for you to accept, Bettina. It's hard for me, too...."

"Hard! I would say that's the understatement of the year. This happens to be my father we're talking about. The father I loved more than any other person on this earth. The man who provided for me, gave me everything I ever wanted. I knew him well. If he had been a thief, I think I would have known it."

Jerry fixed his gray eyes on her, and his voice was a distressed whisper. "You forget, Bettina, I knew him, too. Ever since you and I were kids. And I thought I knew him well. Accepting the truth now isn't exactly easy for me, either. He was like a second father to me."

Bettina took note of the misery on her friend's face. She shook her head. "It can't be true, Jerry. It just can't. I mean, even the fact that they are saying he's alive.... He's been dead for seven years, don't they know that?"

"His body was never found."

Her eyes closed briefly in pain. "That's not the point. If he were alive, he would have contacted me. He would have come back to me. Daddy would never

14 *A Siren's Lure*

have let me believe he was dead. It's...well, it's too cruel even to think about, that's all.''

Jerry reached for her hand. ''Bettina, I'm sorry. I really am. I'll do anything I can to help you.''

She was hurt and angry, and both emotions gave her the excuse to lash out at the closest outlet at hand. ''Why didn't you know before now?'' she snapped. ''This—this spy business you're in. I thought you were supposed to know everything about everybody!''

Jerry's glance ricocheted off the nearby tables. ''Bettina, please!''

She squeezed her eyes shut. ''Oh, damn.'' She opened them and grimaced. ''Jerry, you know I didn't mean to do that.'' They had been close friends for a long time, all of their lives, really, and she had never told any of their mutual friends what he actually did for a living or whom he worked for. It was their secret, theirs to share. ''It's just that I'm so upset. My life is a wreck. Did you know that since the news came out, none of my friends will talk to me? You would think I was some sort of leper.''

''They'll get over it.''

''I don't think so.'' She sniffed derisively. ''Of course, their daddies have all made their millions in tax dodges, fraudulent land schemes, oil swindles. But when my father is labeled a jewel thief, the family name suddenly turns to some sort of blasphemy that must not be uttered in public. I can just hear them whispering behind my back now. 'I always knew there was something strange about that family,' they're saying. 'He looked the type to me,' they're claiming.

A Siren's Lure

'Poor, poor Bettina. Such a pitiful life.' Ooh, just thinking about it makes by blood boil!''

"Good." Jerry smiled. "I'd rather see you indignant than despondent. Quiet desperation doesn't suit you."

She stared at him for a long moment. "You're right. I am damn mad. How could he do this to me? How could he! My own father!''

"So you admit it could be true."

Her chin lifted arrogantly. "I'm not admitting anything." She leaned forward and whispered, "But I'll tell you this—if it is true, the next time I see him I'll kill him myself."

Jerry pursed his lips. "You'll have to find him first. IRS special agents and Interpol have been looking for him, but without much luck so far. Interpol finally put enough facts together to place him at the scene of every major theft, and once the U.S. Treasury Department was brought in and all of his financial records were investigated...well, the pieces just added up to make a pretty convincing picture."

"I'll find him, Jerry," she said firmly.

He tried to hide his smile. "I'm sure you will. But do you want to tell me how?"

"You're such a cynic."

"Just pragmatic, kiddo. If a person doesn't want to be found, there are ways to accomplish that."

"But I'm his daughter."

"I'm sure he has his reasons for not contacting you, for not wanting you involved in this mess."

"Well, it's too late for that. I'm already involved. I don't even have a place to call home anymore." Bet-

16   *A Siren's Lure*

tina leaned closer. "Surely you know people who could...could find him. You know what I mean?"

Jerry took a hefty drink of his scotch. "I doubt very seriously that the Defence Intelligence Agency would list a flamboyant and colorful cat burglar as a top priority." He angled toward her and winked. "Don't forget, there are governments that must be toppled, triple agents to subdue, subversive leaders to assassinate."

"This isn't a joke, Jerry."

"Look, Bettina, I just want you to look at this realistically. If the IRS can't find him, how can you? Where would you even begin?"

She drummed her polished nails against the tabletop. "Well, he supposedly died in Tibet, riding that yak or whatever it was into the mountains."

"That was seven years ago. I don't think he would stay around there. He always hated cold weather. Besides, Le Chat Noir has struck in several cities across Europe in the past year. And, as I said, he almost bought his own ticket to jail last month in Chamonix. He loves to play the gaming houses, Bettina, and that's going to be his own trap sooner or later."

"Le Chat Noir. The Black Cat. How melodramatic!"

"I didn't name him. Interpol did."

"Daddy, Le Chat Noir. It's too much!"

"My point is that you would have no idea where to begin looking for him."

"Okay, so nobody with your agency would be interested enough to try to find him. But what about

A Siren's Lure

someone in the civilian world? Don't you know any private detectives who could look?"

"I know plenty who could look, Bettina, but I just don't know any who could find him. I don't want you wasting what little money you have left."

"I have enough of my own money stuck away that the IRS won't ever find."

His glance shifted away, and he cleared his throat. "You shouldn't tell me that, you know."

"What are you going to do, turn me in?"

He sighed. "What do you think?"

This time, she reached for his hand. "I think you're my friend, Jerry. I need your help."

A waiter hovered nearby, and Jerry glanced up at him. "Are you ready to order, Bettina?"

She shook her head. "I'm not hungry."

Jerry handed the menus back to the waiter. "We'll just finish our drinks and then be on our way."

"Whatever you wish, sir."

Bettina leaned back in her chair and let her eyes sweep across the restaurant. Le Bisque—with its starched linen tablecloths, mosaic-designed ceiling and velvet banquettes along a mirrored wall—catered to the very top layer of the city's social and political cream. She smiled wistfully. "You know, it's funny. I've always taken this opulence and elegance for granted. I've always had money. I guess I assumed I always would."

"Last time we talked, you told me you were getting bored with it all."

"That was when I still had it. It's a completely different story when you don't have it." Jerry laughed at

18　　　　　　　　　*A Siren's Lure*

her honesty. "But it's true," she insisted. "Everything has changed so much in the past few years. All my friends are getting married and having babies."

"I don't think that's as distasteful as you make it sound," he said with a smile.

"Oh? Then how come you're not living in suburbia with a wife, 2.5 kids and a Ford, or whatever it is suburban types drive nowadays?"

"Mercedes. And I haven't had the time."

"Well, neither have I. Nor do I intend to. Once they get married, they don't want to have fun anymore. Where's the excitement? Where's the adventure?"

"Most people don't need as much excitement and adventure in their lives as you do."

Bettina took a slow, thoughtful sip of her drink. "What is it with us, Jerry? Why are we different? You've got adventure with your job. I always had it with Dad and traveling and—"

"And spending money."

This time she took a longer drink, then set the empty glass down and stared into it. "I'm too old to be poor, Jerry. I'll never survive it."

"If you thought you would be poor, you'd marry me. I've only asked you at least thirty times, you know." He chuckled cynically. "I'm not worried about your ending up on skid row, and I don't think you are, either."

She smiled thinly and shook her head. "No, not really. I just wish I understood all of this. If Daddy is alive, I've got to find him. I have to get some answers."

A Siren's Lure 19

"I can't say that I blame you. And I wouldn't mind knowing what has happened to the old bear myself."

"If I found him, you—you wouldn't...well, you know, turn him...Oh, hell, Jerry that was stupid. Of course you wouldn't. I just wish there were someone who was good enough to track him down for me."

"I know a man who is good enough, but—"

"You do?"

Jerry glanced away and, for a brief second, seemed sorry he had said anything. "Well, *knew* him, actually. He's not around anymore."

"Is he dead?"

Jerry swirled the last few drops of scotch in his glass. "Not exactly."

"What is that supposed to mean?"

"It means yes, no, maybe. I'm not sure, but I doubt it. Hell, in fact I know it."

She frowned and laughed at the same time. "Would you like to explain that?"

He let out a slow breath and studied her inquisitive green eyes. "Erickson—that's his name. He is...well, he's kind of like Peter Pan. He'll never grow old and he'll never die. Officially, he's dead, or was, but unofficially...Damn it, Bettina, I've had too many drinks. I always talk too much."

"Not at all." She quickly signaled the waiter to bring them two more drinks before Jerry clammed up on her. "Go on. My interest is definitely piqued."

Jerry didn't argue about the fresh drink that was set in front of him. He took a fortifying draw from it before he spoke. "Upton John Erickson was—is—his name, but the last person who called him Upton

20 *A Siren's Lure*

wound up spending twenty-five hundred dollars for new caps on his teeth." Jerry stared for a long time at his glass, then shook his head. "He was a good friend. And a damn son of a bitch!"

Bettina watched Jerry gulp half his drink down. She wished she knew more about what he did so that she could understand him better. They had been friends forever, yet it seemed she no longer knew him at all. Defense intelligence was all she knew. She was sure he must have a number of past ghosts to contend with, but he had never talked about any of them with her. Until now.

"Tell me about him, Jerry."

He was silent for a few moments, then said, "Erickson was the best damn tracer I've ever known, the best thief—although your dad may be running a close second—and the best con artist."

"I'm shocked, Jerry. I thought you ran only with the straight arrows—the ones waving banners of red, white and blue."

"Don't let his talents fool you. Erickson worked for the government—military intelligence. And as long as it was a covert operation, he was at home, whether it was in the jungles of Nicaragua or in the parlors of France."

"Where did you meet him?"

"Annapolis. He graduated summa cum laude, but he rarely cracked a book. Things that most of us had to bust our tails for came naturally to him."

"Was that where you became good friends?"

"Yeah. He lived down the hall from me. We got to know each other pretty well. After graduation, he trained as a SEAL—"

A Siren's Lure 21

"Seal? Jerry, that's an animal!"

"Not that kind of seal, Bettina. This SEAL stands for sea, air and land tactics—not really an acronym. It's the navy's answer to the Green Beret. SEALs claim to be the best-trained military force in the U.S. and—well, there aren't too many people who would challenge that claim. Anyway, he and his force of elite fighters carried out some legendary exploits in Vietnam. I'm not sure exactly what his official capacity was there, but he was some sort of strategist for top-ranking intelligence officers. I guess it was at this time that his other, more subtle talents became obvious to the government. Meanwhile, I was already pushing a pencil at the DIA."

Bettina tried to read the tone in Jerry's voice. Was he bitter about his own career? Relieved? Frustrated? She couldn't say. "Are you supposed to be telling me all this?"

He regarded her closely, then set down his glass. "Let's go for a walk, okay?"

After Jerry paid the bill, they left the restaurant and headed up the street, following the course of the river. There was no illumination except for the glow of lights from the monuments. Late spring in Washington, D.C., was the best time of the year. The air was soft and full of the rich fragrance of cherry blossoms. They walked quietly beside each other, letting the peaceful night insulate them from the harsher realities of day.

Jerry's hands were thrust deeply into the pockets of his slacks. "You know, Bettina, you're the only one I ever talk to about work—or anything important."

22   *A Siren's Lure*

She looped her arm through his. "I know that. And who do I always go to when I need help or just a big, strong shoulder to cry on?"

He looked down at her and started to speak, but whatever he was about to say was pulled back inside him, where it had always been and where it would always remain. He smiled at her instead.

"Is there a chance this Erickson would help me out?" she asked. "First of all, is he alive or not?"

"Where was I?"

"Vietnam."

"Oh, yeah. Well, after that he did a little bit of everything. We stayed in contact and saw each other whenever we could, but he kept a pretty low profile. It was essential for his job. He helped establish a couple of juntas, aided in training the SEALs who were later involved in the raid on Grenada, tracked down a double agent here and there, then finally was sent to Benin."

Bettina cleared her throat. "Geography, Jerry, is not my best subject. So clue me in, okay?"

"Africa."

"Benin, Africa? Never heard of it. But I'll take your word for it."

"That was in 1980," Jerry continued. "As best as I can decipher the story, he was there to steal some documents—important government contracts—from the home of the country's military leader. Also, the idea apparently was to distract the colonel while a foreign airborne assault took place to overthrow his regime."

"The U.S. wanted this colonel out?"

A Siren's Lure

"Well, actually, it was the French, but we won't talk about that part of it."

"Okay. Go on."

"Anyway, this is where it all gets kind of sketchy. Part of it is purely speculation and part is information that was gathered from other sources on the scene. Somehow, Erickson was captured by soldiers before he could complete the job. He was carted off and sent before the firing squad."

"Oh. I don't think I'm going to like the end of this story."

"No, hang on. It gets really interesting. Something happened—probably the air assault—but whatever it was, it diverted the soldiers' attention, and Erickson, sly fox that he was and is, got away. Instead of heading straight to the border, however, he obviously went back to finish the job he'd been sent to do. We know this because the papers, along with some jewels, were stolen. Erickson is the only one who could have taken them."

"What did he do with them?"

"He probably destroyed the documents. They never surfaced, and that was what was important. The jewels—well, those, I guess, he kept himself. I've been working on this problem for a long time, Bettina, and I still don't have all the answers. But we do know several things. The officer he went down there with—a Major Winston—had been filtering information to the Russians for quite a while. We didn't know it at the time, of course, but we learned about the connection later. We're not sure if Erickson knew or not. I know he wasn't in on it, and the company knows that,

24 *A Siren's Lure*

too...now. At first none of us was sure. You see, Winston was highly respected, an honored war veteran and an influential figure in the agency. But if Erickson figured out what was going on, he might have decided to terminate Winston's arrangement.''

"Terminate? You mean...as in permanently?''

"Terminate, Bettina. Let's just leave it at that. The thing is, Major Winston's car was blown up right outside the colonel's house.''

"Did this man Erickson do it?''

Jerry snorted. "No, not his style at all. But somebody wanted Winston out of the way.''

"And then what happened?''

"Well, the two bodies that were found at the scene were the major's and Erickson's.''

Bettina groaned. "I knew I was going to hate the ending of this story. But how did Erickson...''

"Hold on,'' Jerry said. "It wasn't his body. The dental records finally proved it, but he really had us going there for a while. See, what he did was switch all of his identification with that of this other guy who died in the explosion with Major Winston.''

Bettina grimaced at the thought.

Jerry noticed her expression. "Don't forget,'' he said, "Erickson was a soldier who had seen lots of action. Dead bodies were a dime a dozen in his line of work.''

"But surely when he came home, everyone realized he hadn't died!''

Jerry shook his head. "He never came back. I'm convinced he learned about Winston and thought that he, too, would be suspected of dealing with the Rus-

A Siren's Lure

sians. Nothing else would have made him run like that. Erickson was too good at what he did and, as corny as it may sound to you, he was very loyal to his country. Something scared him badly enough to send him underground for five years.''

''Yes, but you said it was the major who had given the information to the Russians, not Erickson.''

''We know that...now. But you have to understand Erickson. He's never trusted anyone except himself and never depended on anyone else's judgment. At one point, I tracked him to Greece and got a message to him that the agency didn't hold him responsible for Winston's actions. But...well, he didn't believe it. He obviously thought it was a trap. Besides, being a military man, he knows what going AWOL means. He'd be jailed for that, and he's not the type to handle confinement very well.''

''So everyone just gave up on him?''

''Hardly. I've spent a good part of the past four years tracking that bastard. The agency wants him brought in. He knows too much to be out there floating free and wild. They want him inside under the big, fat corporate thumb. Or behind bars is more accurate. He's most likely angry at what happened, and that makes him very unpredictable—which makes the agency very nervous.''

''You said you've been tracking him. Don't you know where he is?''

''Yes and no.''

Bettina glared at her friend. ''You are standing awfully close to the bank of this river to play games with me, Jerry. All it would take is one little shove....''

26 *A Siren's Lure*

"I know, I know. But this is where it gets…sensitive. And I don't mean that in terms of national security, Bettina. I mean it in terms of my own security, jobwise and personal. And yours."

"Mine?"

"Every move you make is being watched. You do realize that, don't you?"

Her eyes widened, and furtively she searched out the shadows that now loomed dark and ominously around them. "What do you mean?"

"Bettina, your father is wanted by a lot of people. You are his daughter. They are going to assume that sooner or later you'll have contact with him. They're going to be watching you and waiting for that moment."

"So if I go looking for this Erickson fellow to help me, and if I find him, you think they'll be right behind me."

"I know so."

She stared straight ahead as the pieces of the puzzle fell together. "And you've looked for him for four years and want to be the one to bring him in, is that right?"

They turned onto the street where her hotel was. Since the government agents had anchored the chain across the front door of her house, the hotel had become her home.

Jerry breathed deeply. "The truth of the matter is, Bettina, I haven't really looked that hard. Oh, I did for a while. I wanted to find him, wanted the promotion that would go along with it. I even wanted to have a drink with the smug bastard. So at first I sniffed be-

A Siren's Lure 27

hind every tree where I thought he might have left his mark. Remember, Erickson was the best tracker I've ever met. He knew all the moves we would make and just how to dodge them. Maybe he finally got tired or I just got better, but about two years ago, I located him in Greece, as I said, and got a message to him to come on in. He didn't go for it and took off shortly after that.

"He's no longer a top priority at the agency. I'm really the only one who's even looking for him. I found out from one of our informants where he's been recently, and if he's still alive and kicking, I'll bet he's there now. If he is and if he does come in, I want it to be with me. But I don't have the time to go after him right now. As I said, he's not a top priority. So if you want to..."

"I understand, Jerry. We can help each other get what we want. I want to find Daddy and you want Erickson."

"Yes. I want you to find your father. I want to know where he is, too. And you're right, I want Erickson. But we've got to work this so that I'm aware of your every move. I want to be on top of it, to be able to get to him before somebody else does. So if you go looking for Erickson, which I know you will, I want to know where you are at all times. On the outside chance that you can find him and convince him to help you, I want to know all your moves to locate your father. In the end, you will lead Erickson to me. Do you understand what I'm saying?"

"I think so."

28 *A Siren's Lure*

"I've spent four years tracking him. Low priority or not, I don't want to lose him now."

"What did you mean about the outside chance that I can convince him? Do you think he won't help me?"

"He wouldn't do it for anyone else, I'm sure of it."

"Why me?"

They had stopped on the sidewalk before the hotel. Jerry tilted his head back and stared up at the stars, smiling. "Why you, indeed." His eyes dropped back to her face. Her blond hair was pale in the moonlight, her slender body elegant in the gray cashmere coat. "I know you well, Bettina. And, no offense, but I seriously doubt that you've ever been denied anything your precious little heart desired. I don't think you'll be satisfied until you have him hook, line and sinker."

She smiled, not about to deny Jerry's quite accurate analysis of her character. "Are you going to tell me where this former war hero is?"

"Capri."

"The island?"

"Yes. Actually, he was last seen in Anacapri, going under the name of John Stewart. I'm not sure which village he's living in, though."

"You'll furnish me with a photograph and all the necessary biographical info, I assume."

Jerry laughed. "If you ever need a job, Bettina, we could use you. Poor Erickson. If he only knew what you had in store for him, he'd probably head straight for Madagascar."

"And I'd be right behind him."

"I don't doubt that for a minute, Bettina Bacheller. But keep in mind that four or five other determined agencies will be right behind you."

She smiled. "Yes, but as long as I can stay a step ahead..."

"You always have, Bettina. A step ahead of all of us."

Jerry watched her walk into the bright lobby of the hotel, leaving him standing on the dark sidewalk. She was the only woman he had ever wanted. And the one woman he would never have.

He turned toward the street and hailed a taxi to take him home.

Chapter Three

Alvin Bilgeworth leaned back in his worn leather chair. His feet were propped up on the Formica desk, his little toe poking a hole through the vinyl shoes. While a toothpick was working at the lunch in his teeth, he studied the file in his lap, the one labeled in pencil: Bacheller.

He ran his tongue over his teeth and made a loud sucking noise as he flipped through his handwritten notes. He didn't really need the notes, for he had all the information tucked away in his head, where it counted. Yessiree, old Alvin had it all upstairs. In one dusty cubbyhole of his brain was a list of every stolen item that had been attributed to Le Chat Noir, and next to each item was its declared value. Especially that diamond necklace belonging to Mrs. Clarence Stanhope.

Come hell or high water, he was determined to recover that necklace and receive a ten percent finder's fee from Hopkins Mutual. So you could bet your sweet keister he knew Stephen Bacheller. He knew to the penny how much the old guy had left to that daughter of his, and he had memorized the dollar fig-

A Siren's Lure 31

ure that the IRS claimed the Bacheller estate owed the United States government.

Alvin tossed the shredded toothpick toward the trash can, but it missed its mark and landed on the floor beside the latest unpaid electric bill. He opened his desk drawer and pulled out a jar of peanuts, unscrewing the lid and popping ten or fifteen nuts in his mouth at once.

Yep, old Alvin had a head for figures; he knew almost everything there was to know about that classy Bacheller broad. Size eight dress, seven and a half shoe, thirty-four B in the headlights. He had figured out how many times a week she went out on dates, then had calculated to a mathematic precision that she saw a guy 2.486 times before dumping him flat for a new man. She certainly wasn't one to let any grass grow under her feet.

And, most important of all, he knew exactly how much she had paid yesterday for her first-class ticket to Rome, as well as the departure time of the flight and her assigned seat number.

He tossed back another handful of peanuts and spit out a hard husk that had gotten mixed in with them. Bettina Bacheller didn't know it, but she was going to lead him straight to that ten percent reward.

Alvin Bilgeworth smiled most unpleasantly, smacked his lips and polished off the jar of dry-roasted.

BETTINA STOOD on the crowded dock of Marina Grande, a Louis Vuitton suitcase in her hand. Her father had never brought her to Capri. She wondered now if he had ever been here on his own. What places

32 *A Siren's Lure*

had he gone to that he had never told her about? What things had he done? What crimes had he...?

After every trip, they had sat in his study and he had told her all about the museums, the beaches, the homes in which he had been entertained and the people he had met, the priceless art objects he had bought...

Bought. Le Chat Noir didn't buy things. He stole them.

Bettina suddenly realized she was blocking someone's path, so she shifted her bag to the other hand and stepped away from the *aliscafo* that had brought her from Naples to the island. The crowded port was jammed with motor boats, rowboats, yachts and small steamers. The smells of fuel in the air and dead fish in the bay forced her to move even faster. Ahead, white rocky cliffs, like rough-hewn seawalls, thrust upward from the green hills and fell down into a sea that was in spots blue and in others a brilliant emerald-green. Fishermen's houses, in soft colors of white, coral and yellow, and built like steps up the mountain, were niched together like pieces of a jigsaw puzzle.

The sky was a clear blue, with not a cloud in sight, and the sun felt warm against her face. Hearing the excited voices and laughter along the port, Bettina felt a buoyancy within her that she had not felt for a long time. The sky and the sea were blue, the scent of orange blossoms was full and heavy, and a flock of sea gulls frolicked in the air above the beach.

The perfection of the moment wrapped itself around her, whisking away the anger and doubts she had been harboring about her father's treachery. How could he have let her believe he was dead all these years? No matter what he had done, though, he was still her father. And she was going to find him. But first she had to locate the elusive Mr. Erickson. Once she had him, they would go after her father together. She would get what she wanted, and in the end, Jerry would get what he wanted. It was a perfect arrangement.

Jerry's briefing ran through her mind once again. "Erickson may not even look like this anymore, Bettina. I want you to be prepared for anything." Just two days ago, he had shown her the second photograph he had of Erickson, which had been taken six months before. Jerry was right; the man looked nothing like the one in the first picture. The younger Erickson, the one who had been sent to Benin and then had "died," had sandy-brown hair, blue eyes and a clean-shaven face. The Erickson who had last been seen in Anacapri, living under the name of John Stewart, had very dark brown hair, brown eyes and a mustache.

"Hair dye, contacts and a mustache can do wonders," Jerry had said. "His mannerisms have changed, of course, as well as his name and who knows what else. The man's good at this sort of thing. He wanted a new life, and he got it."

"And this place where he was seen?" she had asked.

"He frequents a bar in Punta Azzurra. Caffè Solare. It's out of Anacapri, on the far side of the island. You may have to ask, but I think you'll be able to find it."

"I'm sure I will."

"Bettina..."

34 *A Siren's Lure*

"Will you stop worrying about me, Jerry? Everything is going to be fine, you'll see."

"But he's unpredictable."

"So is my life at this point. I can handle it *and* him."

"Don't forget to look behind you, too. You have the number where you can reach me?"

"Yes."

"Day or night, Bettina."

"I know. I'll call. I promise."

That had been two days ago, at the airport. Now she was standing in the port of Capri, studying Erickson's picture again. A group of Italian soldiers circled her and whistled low between their teeth, but she ignored them as she concentrated on the photograph in her hands. The picture had been taken with a telephoto lens, but Erickson's image was clear. He had a tan and seemed completely at ease with his surroundings. He didn't at all look like a man who had been hiding from himself and the world for five years.

According to the biographical information Jerry had provided, Erickson was thirty-seven years old. His hobbies were women and scuba diving. Trained as a navy SEAL, he was probably very good at the latter. And if he was as handsome as the photograph indicated, he was no doubt very successful with the former.

Bettina slipped the picture back into the manila envelope and put it in her purse. She looked around for a taxi, but all were occupied just then. Since she didn't want to wait around in this crowd for another cab, she walked into one of the beachfront shops and asked how far it was to the Grand Hotel Quisisana. When

A Siren's Lure 35

she was quite young, her father had insisted that she learn as many languages as possible; now she was fluent in Spanish and French, and her Italian was passable. She had to ask the shopkeeper to repeat his answer, but on the second go-around she understood. A funicular, it seemed, was only a half block away, and for only five hundred lire—or approximately twenty-five American cents—it would take her up to the center of Capri. From there she would have to walk to her hotel. But even if she were to find an available taxi driver, the shopkeeper assured her that the car could take her no farther than the funicular would.

She left the shop, walked the half block, and immediately boarded the cable train without a wait. With its windows open to the spring day, it rose at a steady pace, cutting a thin path through lush groves of oranges and lemons. Purple bougainvillea grew in thick abundance along the mountain track, and little winding pathways that led off to summer villas were lined with oleanders and nasturtiums. The island was a sculptured geological phenomenon. Nature had patiently carved the rough, calcareous rock into sharp peaks and hollowed grottos, and had sliced thousands of ravines into the island from every angle.

Bettina had been lucky that life had afforded her the time and money to travel. She had never tired of seeing new places, trying different foods and speaking in other languages. Of course, now all that might have to change. She had enough money stuck away in different accounts to tide her over for a little while, but once that was gone, she would have to alter her life drastically. But no, she wasn't going to dwell on that too

36 *A Siren's Lure*

much right now. She would worry about it if and when the time came and not before. For now, she had enough to worry about just finding her father.

If he were really this internationally famous jewel thief, what could have driven him to start a life of crime? Or had he always been a thief? She had assumed—he had claimed—that he was in the import-export business. Stephen Bacheller certainly did not have to steal to support his family. He had come from wealth and married into it. His father had owned several important hotels before selling out to one of the large chains. Bettina's mother had been the only child of a flamboyant man who had published a respected magazine and countless prize-winning novels. Money had flowed freely from both sides of the family, and if Stephen Bacheller had decided never to engage in a day's worth of work, he and Bettina still would have lived among the pleasure-seeking rich.

Beyond that was the burning question of why he had to make his own daughter think he was dead. Why had that been so necessary? Couldn't he have told her the truth? Wouldn't she have accepted it?

No, she wasn't really sure that she would have accepted it any better from him than she was trying to accept it now.

The funicular jolted to a stop at the top of the mountain, and the doors slip open. Bettina stepped off and climbed the steep stairs up to the square. Colorful umbrellas were shading outdoor cafés. By summer, the piazza would be so crowded that one would barely be able to move about. But now it was relatively empty. Only a few people sat around drinking

A Siren's Lure 37

wine or bargained in the small shops for leather shoes or lacquered music boxes.

Bettina asked a shopkeeper for directions to the Quisisana and then began the quarter-mile hike through streets that wound along the ancient rocks they were built upon. Hawkers stood in the doorways of their shops and beckoned her inside, hoping to sell her a pretty bauble. She declined them all with a smile as she moved on toward her hotel.

The suitcase was beginning to weigh heavily and slow her down. She changed hands several times when her fingers started to cramp. At every turn there were cafés, lined with pots of geraniums and covered with trellises that were laden with drooping pink bougainvillea. The scent of the flowers was intoxicating.

It had been hours since Bettina had eaten breakfast in Naples, and she was ready for food and some of that rare and delicious wine that was bottled from Capri's own vineyards. She rounded another curve onto the Via Camerelle and saw her hotel in front of her. The Quisisana was painted in a soft, pale yellow, with white awnings gracing the entrance. Outside the front door was a terrace with tables and chairs.

Bettina walked across the black-tiled lobby and registered at the desk. A bellman was immediately beside her to help with her luggage.

"You should have told us when you would arrive, signorina. We would have had someone meet you at the Marina and bring you here."

"Thank you," she said, "but I really wasn't sure what time I would be arriving. I took the funicular, and it was quite adequate."

38 *A Siren's Lure*

Her room was lovely, done in the clean simplicity of white, for which Capri was famous. It had bare wood floors that glistened with fresh polish and a double bed with a flowered bedspread. French doors with coral shutters led out to a tiled terrace, on which stood huge pots of flowers and a wrought-iron table and chairs.

She unpacked her bag and tried to decide what she would do first to find John Erickson. She was staying in Capri only because this hotel had been so highly recommended, but if Jerry was correct, Erickson lived in Anacapri, the village up at the top of the island. It was too late today to do anything, but first thing tomorrow she would start showing his photograph around in the hope that someone would recognize him and point her in his direction. If that didn't work, she would sit in the bar on Punta Azzura and wait until he showed up. But somehow, she was going to find him.

She left her room and went down to the lobby, where she found doors leading out to the gardens and pool. She stood on the far deck beyond the pool and gazed down at the blue Tyrrhenian. The vineyards and oranges groves below were terraced to the sea. Wild cliffs led down to Marina Piccola and the gardens of Augustus; beyond the gardens stood the famous Faraglioni, three statuesque rocks that protruded upward from the water like a gateway into the sea.

It was a purely physical moment, with the smells and sights and sounds all wrapped up in a symphonic whole—the kind of moment that often gave one a false sense of security. The kind that now had Bettina Bacheller firmly believing that all would be right with her world once again.

Chapter Four

"Buon giorno." Erickson smiled at the dark, round woman behind the fruit cart.

"Ah, buon giorno, signore." She watched him pick up an orange. "These oranges are very good. Ripe and sweet."

"Bene! I'll take six, *per favore."*

The woman picked out six of the best and put them in a sack for him. He paid, and she smiled sweetly at him.

It was another beautiful morning, like most of them on this island. The colors, the scents, the happy, animated people—all insulated him against the world he wanted to stay away from. He was content here. He was alone. No one came bothering him. If he wanted friends, he knew where to find them. If he wanted women, there were plenty available. Even the military had stopped looking for him. A few years ago, things had been different. Then, everywhere he had gone and every move he had made were being traced. He had known it, and he had known who was behind it. Jerry McCluskey. But he hadn't been hounded for a long time now, and he wondered why. Surely they hadn't

40   *A Siren's Lure*

given up on bringing him in. That wasn't the way the outfit worked. If they wanted someone in, they didn't stop until they had him. Erickson assumed that sooner or later somebody would catch up with him, too. He just didn't know when.

After buying the fruit, he left the piazza and headed down a narrow, winding street. At the end was a small shop in which he purchased a couple of bottles of Rubesco Riserva '75, a plumlike Umbrian wine that he was particularly fond of. Next door to this shop, he bought a couple of loaves of bread and a hunk of pecorino cheese.

He stopped to talk for a few minutes with each of the shopkeepers before heading back to his secluded house on the hill. That afternoon, he would take his scuba gear and climb down the rocks for a dive. And tomorrow...well, he would decide what he wanted to do then. When he had been a soldier of war, he had taken each day as it came. One day at a time. He saw no reason not to do the same now. One day at a time.

"As long as it was a covert operation, he was at home, whether it was in the jungles of Nicaragua or in the parlors of France."

Looking at him now, Bettina could see that Jerry had been right. This man Erickson would fit in anywhere. Actually, he was much more handsome than his photograph had indicated. He had that same relaxed air about him, the look of a man who had found his niche in life and was now content. But his face wore the texture of one who had spent more time in the jungles than in any parlors. And he hadn't molded those broad shoulders from years of nothing but so-

A Siren's Lure 41

cial repartee and parlor games. His was a body that had been stressed to the physical limits.

It was the third time she had come to the Caffè Solare, hoping to find him there. She had been showing his photograph around the island, but without much success. No one seemed to recognize him, or if anyone did, she was not told about it. Perhaps the people she asked assumed she was a jilted lover or a wife seeking a wayward husband. But whatever the reason, no one had pointed her in the direction of the man now living under the name of John Stewart.

So she had wandered the labyrinthine streets of Anacapri, passing old houses built with thick, whitewashed walls or painted in soft pastel colors. Soon the winding footpath left the village behind and opened up into the vineyards and the ubiquitous orange and lemon orchards that covered the slopes. She had hiked down across the fields until the path dropped with the cliffs in a sharp incline, a narrow walkway almost hidden by the thick vegetation and the natural stone arches formed by wind and water through the rocks. The salty smell of the sea and the cry of sea gulls had accompanied her to the iron gate of the secluded café.

Built into the side of the cliff, Caffè Solare was as lovely and peaceful as the island on which it sat. Open to the elements, it was covered only by wooden latticework laced with bougainvillea. The tables, chairs and fence that surrounded it were wrought iron. Flowers were everywhere, red and coral and white blooms climbing the fence and the rustic pillars that held up the lattice roof. The fragrance of orange blossoms filled the air; from the stereo the sounds of a Scarlatti overture wound through the pine trees.

42 *A Siren's Lure*

And now, on her third day, Erickson had finally appeared.

She was sitting at a table near the entrance, close enough to see over the cliffs to the clear, green depths below. She had just about given up hope of his coming when she saw a lone figure walking down the pathway. Her breath caught for a second or two while she made sure in her own mind that he was the right man. It could have been wishful thinking. She had watched every man who came through that gate with the hope that he would be Erickson. But this time she didn't need to recheck the photograph.

He was dressed in poplin trousers that were gathered at the waist and ankles, and a loose-fitting cotton shirt. Very Italian, she decided. Not at all the look of a soldier who had crawled around the swamps and jungles of the warring world. His hair was dark, almost black, and he had a thick mustache, but his sunglasses hid the color of his eyes. Still, there was no mistaking the man from the photograph. He had the same solid but casual air about him, the same confident angle of jaw and breadth of shoulder.

Bettina watched him amble across the terrazzo floor and take a seat at a table about twenty feet away. She leaned back in her chair and shifted her eyes toward the sea. She had to approach this very carefully. The timing had to be perfect, the mood just so. She had to ensnare him with her bait and make sure he was hooked. Her performance would have to be supreme.

The waiter brought him a glass of wine and then came to her table with a bowl of ripe olives in thick oil.

A Siren's Lure

"Per favore, could you tell me what wine that gentleman ordered?" Her Italian was slow and labored, but the meaning was clear enough to the waiter.

"That man?"

"Yes."

"Lacrima Cristi. A very good selection, signorina. Would you like to try some?"

Bettina's small smile was cunning. "No, but please bring a full bottle to the gentleman's table and give me the bill."

"Very good, signorina."

Bettina, quite pleased with herself but at the same time a little nervous, sat back in her chair once more and studied the scenery around her. A sea gull flew onto a rock and then dove in a graceful arc down to the water far below. The music of Scarlatti had given way to Mascagni's "Intermezzo," and a light breeze stirred the rhythm of the pine needles.

In the periphery of her eye, she saw the bottle being brought to Erickson's table. She held her breath and the waiter bent down to tell him that the young woman at the far table had bought it for him.

Erickson had removed his sunglasses, and now his eyes met hers across the café. He lifted his glass in a salute and gave her a slight nod. Responding with an artful smile in return, she then forced herself to look away.

After a moment's hesitation, he stood up and carried the bottle, his glass and an empty glass off the serving cart over to her table.

"Such generosity should be shared, don't you agree?"

44 *A Siren's Lure*

His Italian was flawless, but she knew she wouldn't be able to fool him with hers, so she responded in English.

"I understand it's a wonderful wine," she said.

He sat down across from her and poured the dry, white wine into her glass. "Oh, it is," he said in English. "Tear of Christ. That's what it's called. The grapes are grown on the slopes of Vesuvius."

She tasted it. "It's very nice."

He sat back in his chair and crossed an ankle over his knee, breathing deeply of the salt-sea air mixed with the heady scent of orange.

"This is a lovely spot," she said.

"Yes, it is. Very secluded. *Molto tranquillo.*" He stared pointedly at her. "Not too many tourists find this place."

She smiled enigmatically. "Then I suppose I am one of the exceptional ones."

He watched her closely, but lifted his glass. "To an exceptional woman."

They drank in silence for a moment. The afternoon didn't call for much talk. Its rhythm was slow and gentle, like the music.

"I'm John Stewart," he finally said. "And you?"

"Bettina Bacheller."

His chest expanded as if he were absorbing her name with all of his senses, as if he were touching her and smelling the fragrance of her perfume. It was an exhilarating notion, and she was aware of a chill of anticipation sliding along the length of her arms. "Have you been on the island long?"

"No, I just arrived this morning."

A Siren's Lure 45

His eyes narrowed. "And you already have found your way to Punta Azzurra. Amazing."

She stared back at him. His eyes were a soft terracotta brown, like the earth after a spring rain. Fertile, potent, rich...and a bit savage. But she tossed her hair back over her shoulder, refusing to show any signs of nervousness. "I'm one of those who like to take the unbeaten path."

"Apparently so."

"I'm touring the coast of Italy," she said with the most innocent smile she could muster. "I landed in Rome a couple of days ago, and after I leave here, I'll take a car along the Amalfi drive and then go back up north. I'd like to drive as far as Genoa."

"You're traveling alone?"

She met his direct stare. "Yes."

This time his glass was raised in a silent, somehow more intimate toast. "If you arrived only this morning, you must not have had a chance to see much of the island...except, of course, the untrod path from Caprile."

"That's true, and there is so much I want to see. The Blue Grotto, the Certosa of San Giacomo, the gardens of Augustus. I've seen only the outside of the Church of San Michele."

"How long are you planning to stay here?"

"That all depends."

"On what?"

She smiled coyly and took a sip of her wine. "On who invites me to stay."

His surprise lasted a mere second as he cocked his head in astute appraisal. "You don't waste much time on preliminaries, do you?"

46   *A Siren's Lure*

Slowly she began to caress the stem of her wineglass. "I've found that there is much more to life than preliminaries."

His expression did not change. "Have you, now?"

"Have you been on the island very long?" she asked, breaking the more intimate moment with perfect calculation.

He studied her closely before answering. "A few years."

"And before that?"

"I've lived all over."

"How exciting. What do you do for a living?"

"I'm a consultant."

"Oh? What do you consult about?"

"International business, primarily. I help companies do business in foreign countries."

"That must be very interesting."

"Not really," he said, his expression bland.

She gave a sudden laugh at his honesty.

"And you?" he asked, spinning her thoughts around. "What do you do?"

"I don't work."

"I didn't think so." He shrugged at her quick glance. "As you said, you're not the beaten-path type."

She took a slow, steadying breath and focused on the pine trees as their branches danced and swayed in the breeze to Musetta's Waltz. "Speaking of paths," she said, smiling, "where does that one lead?" She pointed down the hill toward the sea.

"It goes down about a quarter of a mile to a point where you can see the Faraglioni. Have you seen them yet?"

A Siren's Lure 47

"No, but I want to."

"Now is the best time of day, when they are resting against the sunset. Are you tired of walking?"

"Oh, no, I love to walk."

He didn't argue or seem overwhelmed when Bettina paid the check. She wasn't really surprised. He obviously knew his way around wealthy women—around all kinds of women.

They left the café together and headed down the steep, rocky path. It wound through the trees and flowering shrubs; in places it was more like ancient carved steps across the sharp terrain than an actual walkway. Stonecrop grew between the rocks on one side; on the other was the gray-green broom with its yellow, sweet-pea-shaped flowers. The sun was low in the sky. A coral light rippled across the surface of the water, and the scent of lemon filled the air. Goat tracks led off from the main path and headed up into cliffs that were so steep that no man could climb them without ropes, carabiners and pitons.

Bettina and Erickson stopped at the edge of the cliff. To the south, they could see the giant, moss-covered rocks that rose like ancient battlements from the sea. The sun was behind the Faraglioni, which gave off a mystical glow and seemed to have a golden fire burning deep within them.

Bettina tried to take in all the magical splendor of the scenery before her, behind her and all around. "It is so beautiful here, I may never leave!" she exclaimed.

"That's the lure of the island. Once you experience its specialties, you are captured. Are you familiar with the legend of the Sirens?"

48 *A Siren's Lure*

"Only what little I recall from reading Homer." She turned toward him with a conquettish smile. "And that was a few years ago. Is this the island he was describing?"

"Yes. There are several accounts of it, actually, in both the Odyssey and in the story of Jason and the Argonauts."

He was standing behind her now as she gazed out over the sea, and his rough, male voice held all the mystery and enchantment of the island.

"As Ulysses was returning home from his odyssey, the goddess Circe warned him about the isle of the Sirens. These nymphs, these muses of death, charmed sailors with their lovely songs, luring the ships into the rocks and therefore into certain death. Circe instructed Ulysses to stop up the ears of his seamen with wax so that they could not hear the sweet strains of music. He was to have himself bound to the mast and not to be released, no matter how much he begged, until his ship had safely passed the island."

Bettina noticed a slight shift in the tone of Erickson's voice, as if he might be warning himself to heed Circe's admonishment, but then maybe that was only her own conscience prodding her. She looked down at the varying shades of pink in the water, broken by the looming shadows of the darkening cliffs. "You can almost hear it, can't you?" She sighed. "The sounds coming through the trees and skimming along the rocks seem like music."

His voice was low and gravelly. "Yes. It's like a song. Soft and seductive."

She turned around and saw that he was watching her. He was terribly handsome. The brown of his eyes

A Siren's Lure 49

was like a warm, moist patch of earth she could lie in. But she had to shake off that feeling. He did not really have brown eyes. Those were just contacts. He didn't really have dark hair. Nor was his name John Stewart. She had to remember who he was and what she was there for. Standing here on the cliffs of the Sirens, he had a powerful and fascinating lure of his own, but she must not be pulled in by it. He was a man who had lived through hell and who had probably killed many times to survive. He had carved out a new life for himself and would not easily give it up. His quiet, gentle demeanor now was a charade, just as his eyes were, and his hair, and the rest of his new life. Underneath it all, he was a soldier—no doubt, a deadly one.

She looked back at the Faraglioni and shivered.

"Cold?" he asked.

"A little. Should we head back up before it gets dark?" Already the path in front of her was hidden in the shadows of evening. The dark trees arched over the stone pathway and gave a menacing cover that only a few minutes earlier had been charming.

"If you would like to." His voice was curiously flat.

They started the long climb upward, Bettina walking just ahead of Erickson. She hated these ominous sensations she was now having, but she couldn't keep them away. They inched along her skin and slid up her spine. She kept feeling him behind her; she was aware of his every footfall; she could hear his breath, even and composed despite the steady uphill climb. It was as if she might turn around and find him looming larger than life on the pathway. Deadly scenarios kept playing over in her mind, macabre games of "what

50   *A Siren's Lure*

if.'' What if she were cast into the sea? No one would ever find her. What if she were buried among the brushes of broom? How long would it be before another traveler on a solitary trek in this out-of-the-way spot came across her broken body?

His voice behind her made her jump and spin around. "What did you say?"

He caught the anxiety in her voice and eyes, but kept his own voice controlled. "I said I wish I had a jacket for you. You're shaking like a leaf. I didn't realize it was getting so cool."

"Oh...no, I'm fine, really I am." She turned around and continued up the narrow trail. To her acute relief, they finally reached the iron gate of the café. But she still had a long way to go before she could get to Anacapri and a taxi that could take her back down to the security of her hotel in the lower village.

"Why are you staying in Capri instead of up here?" he asked after he had found out how far she had to travel.

"The Quisisana was recommended to me. I didn't know where else to stay."

"It's definitely the best hotel on the island—that is, if you happen to enjoy hanging around with the smart international set."

She caught his lazily crooked grin and smiled back. The man had a sense of humor, after all.

"But," he continued, "it all depends on where you want to spend your time. It's much more crowded down there."

"I know." She breathed in the softness of the evening. The fears were fading fast and now seemed irrational to her. She wasn't usually so skittish, nor had she ever been afraid of much of anything in her life. She wasn't about to let her imagination get the best of her now. "It's so lovely up here. I hate to leave. However..." She sighed and turned toward the road leading back to the village.

"Yes," he murmured, then led her away from the café, the cliffs and the seductive lure of the Sirens.

Within half an hour, she was climbing into the back of a long red convertible with one of Capri's sadistically amused, daredevilish drivers at the wheel. Erickson helped her in, then rested his strong, tanned arms on the door.

"Why don't you come for dinner tomorrow night?"

Bettina lifted her eyes to his face, excited with the way things were going so far. She had been her most charming self on the walk back to the village. She knew she had to capture his interest first, make him want to see more of her, and then—and only then— she would hit him with the true purpose of her visit to his island. Her pose now was one of sultry nonchalance. "Dinner," she repeated.

"Yes, at my house. I'm a reasonably good cook, and you can't leave the island until you try the prawns. We're famous for them."

She angled her body toward him. "A must for the tourist, is it?"

He leaned a little closer to her and answered smoothly, "Absolutely. Puts all the rest of the island's legends to shame."

"Well, then..."

"Good," he concluded, rapping the side of the door with his palm. "I'll have a driver pick you up at your hotel at eight."

52 *A Siren's Lure*

She tried to study him coolly, but it was difficult. He was really too close to her. He was also very dominant, very sturdy, very male. But she had to maintain the upper hand. It was the only way. "Make it eight-thirty."

She tapped the driver's shoulder, and the taxi sped off at breakneck speed around the hairpin curves. Erickson was left standing in her presumptuous wake. Bettina leaned back in the seat, holding on to the side of the door for balance, and smiled hugely. She had him. He had gone for the bait. Tomorrow she would haul him in, hook, line and sinker.

She refused to listen to the tiny voice inside that told her it might just be the other way around.

Chapter Five

Bettina had tried to keep herself occupied throughout the day, but it had not been easy. She spent the morning walking up and down the narrow, winding streets of Li Campi and Le Botteghe, and she shopped in some of the boutiques on Vittorio Emanuele.

A couple of times during the morning, she had the strangest sensation that someone was watching her or following her. But she brushed it off as nothing more than pure fantasy. Jerry had filled her head with too many warnings about everyone watching her to see if she contacted her father. Paranoia, that was all it was.

In the afternoon, she walked all the way to the medieval monument of the Certosa of San Giacomo and to Augustus Park. But all she could think about was what she would say to Erickson that night, how he would react, what she would do to convince him to help her. Maybe feminine wiles would be enough to win him over, but she didn't really think so. He had been too cautious for too many years to succumb to something as nebulous as a woman's charm. She had thought about the direct approach, appealing to his sense of honor and duty to his fellow American. But

54 *A Siren's Lure*

she didn't believe that would work, either. A man who had switched identification with a dead man was a few degrees beyond the God, Mother and Country stage.

When she arrived back at the hotel, she had a couple of hours to get ready, so she sat at one of the outdoor tables, drank a glass of Frascati and ate a few of the olives and walnuts that were provided at each table. She still had to call Jerry, but for some reason, she had been putting it off. She tried hard to relax and not to think of her father. She tried to make herself believe that she was on some kind of impersonal mission. She had gotten used to his death and to being without him. Though she still missed him terribly, she did not want to risk too much in the way of expectations, merely to be left with nothing but disappointment in the end.

ONLY ONE LAMP was on in the living room, and it didn't give off much light. The evening shadows had slithered across the stone floor and lay in wait for the moon's illumination.

He sat on the couch and smoked, waiting. The house was built on the edge of a jagged cliff that dropped fifty or so feet to a plateau of ferns and moss, fell away again to a terraced field of orange and lemon trees, then finally plunged downward to the sea. Beyond the windows, he could see nothing but blackness. Once the moon came up, the sea would take on a unearthly blue color, and tiny pinpoints of light from houses and from lanterns in the cafés and trattorias would flicker across the island like fireflies on a summer night.

A Siren's Lure 55

He stubbed out his cigarette and immediately lit another one. Soon she would be here. Bettina Bacheller was a beautiful woman. Thick blond hair flowed over her shoulders in soft waves. Rich-girl hair, the kind that was accustomed to salon treatments and lots of expensive pampering. And her body—it, too, had been pampered. She had ivory skin, a switch from the darker, olive-skinned women he had been with since living here. Green eyes, catlike. A very seductive smile. Great figure.

He took a deep breath and let it out slowly. She would be here in just a little while.

He glanced down at the cushion of the couch on which he was sitting and ran his hand over the smooth shaft of the automatic pistol. After a pause, he picked up the gun, released the magazine catch and shoved in the cartridge clip. He inspected the safety, then set the pistol down beside him. He checked his watch. Eight forty-five. If she had been ready on time, she would be here within fifteen minutes.

He waited.

"TELL ME EVERYTHING, Bettina."

She knew now why she had put off calling Jerry. He was going to squeeze out every drop of energy she had left with his questions. But she took a deep breath and began, relating every detail of the past two days on the island and her encounter with Erickson.

"You're sure it was he?"

"Positive, Jerry."

"How does he look?"

"Good. Very handsome."

56 *A Siren's Lure*

There was a slim space of silence. "That's not what I meant, Bettina. I meant does he appear cautious or overly confident, or did he slip and make any careless mistakes in conversation? Anything like that."

"No, no mistakes. He seemed a bit cautious at first, but—well, I think I have put that to rest. He doesn't have a clue that I know who he is. He's convinced that I'm a wealthy, independent woman traveling the country on my own."

"When do you see him again?"

"Tonight."

"Oh?"

"Yes, he invited me for dinner. Tonight I'm going to confront him with what I know. And I'll ask for his help in finding Daddy."

"You're sure he doesn't suspect you?"

"Positive, Jerry. You've got to stop worrying."

"I can't, Bettina. You don't know him. Even I don't know him anymore. I don't know how desperate he is. That can be a very dangerous position."

"I'll be fine—really, I will."

"I want you to call me when you get back to your hotel tonight, do you understand?"

Bettina laughed. "Is this some sort of bed check, Jerry?"

"Joke if you like, but I'm serious. I want to make sure you're back safely in your hotel."

"Okay, Papa Bear, okay. I'll call. Now stop fretting."

After she had hung up, she was thoroughly exhausted...she felt as if she had been through some political debriefing under hot lights. Jerry was such a

A Siren's Lure 57

worrywart. His problem was that he had been in this spy business for too long. He no longer trusted anyone.

To rid her mind of the cat-and-mouse routine, she took a leisurely bath, dressed and went down to the lobby to wait for her driver. He was right on time. They walked the quarter mile to the piazza where he had left his car. Then began the death-defying drive to the village at the top of the island.

He stopped the car in the center of Vittoria Square. From there, he escorted her on foot down through San Nicola Square and turned into the Via Le Boffe. The gentleman's house, he informed Bettina, was just past Caprile.

She had walked that way yesterday to the Punta Azzurra, so she was sure she could find it, but the driver insisted on accompanying her. Signor Stewart had instructed him to do so. Once they left the maze of houses behind, the man pointed to Stewart's house in the distance. It was out on a point, by itself, tucked into a grove of pines. Just to the right of it was an orchard of orange trees.

Bettina thanked the driver and insisted that he leave her there. She would just as soon walk the rest of the way by herself. It was only another quarter of a mile, and she needed the time to clear her mind of any doubts about what she was going to do.

Of course, she knew exactly what she was going to do. She was going to clean up the mess in which her father had left her. She was going to find him and get some answers to the hundreds of questions she now had about his past, his present and his future. Her own

58   *A Siren's Lure*

future was at stake here, too, and she was not going to go back to Washington without a clear-cut sense of what that future held for her.

As far as Erickson was concerned, she would do whatever she had to do to get him to help her find her father, and if it took blackmail to force some altruism out of him...well, she was certainly not above that.

She thought of how he had looked yesterday afternoon on the cliff, staring out over the Faraglioni, and of the way the setting sun had lingered in his eyes and hair. She remembered every nuance of his voice as he had related the story of the Sirens. There was depth in his voice and, she felt sure, a full range of untapped emotions.

She realized she had stopped in the pathway, at once unsure of the steps she must take tonight to secure his help. Once he found her father, she was planning to lead Erickson into a trap, the one she and Jerry had set out for him. But she had to find her father, and if this was the only way...

She was standing in a small clearing within fifty yards of his house. The thick, white-washed walls were cracked in spots, and an ancient rock path led to a stone archway. She forced her feet to continue forward, repeating to herself all the reasons for her being here. At this point in her life, she had no other choice.

She approached the house, walked under the archway and found herself in a small courtyard. Large pots were filled with flowers and ferns; a shade tree rose from the center of the garden.

A Siren's Lure   59

The front entrance, too, was a stone archway, with a carved wooden door in its frame. She took several deep breaths before raising her hand to knock. The time was at hand. *Go for it, Bettina.* When her knuckles lifted and rapped against the wood, the door gave way. By the touch of her hand alone, it swung partially open on its hinges. No one had opened it from the inside.

Only a dim shaft of light angled through the aperture and she hesitated, wondering if she should knock again. But instead, she carefully pushed the door open farther and stepped into the darkened tiled entryway.

"John? Hello. Is anyone home?" Gooseflesh rose along her arms and against the back of her neck. This was not the way she had expected to be greeted, and her lungs automatically sucked in a sudden breath of caution. Maybe Jerry had been right. After all, what did she really know about this man?

Nothing. She knew absolutely nothing about him.

She should leave.

Right away.

The moment the thought entered her mind, the heavy wooden door slammed shut behind her.

She spun around.

From the gray shadows, Erickson stepped forward and rammed his back against the wood to make sure the door was closed tightly.

"*Buona sera*, Miss Bacheller. Or is that even your real name?"

She froze, her breath caught in a lump at the base of her throat, fear clamping like a vise around her stomach. She stared at him, unable to answer. He was only about five feet away. And her eyes were stuck stupidly on his hands.

For it was the first time in her life that anyone had ever pointed a gun at her.

Beyond that, she was positive that he planned to use it.

Chapter Six

She tried to catch her breath. She tried to find her voice. But both were stuck in her throat, holding her paralyzed in the airless void. Her eyes lifted to his face. It was cold, hard, unyielding. Fixed. And the worst part of it all was that her brain, too, seemed paralyzed. For she could not remember his name, not his assumed one, not his real one. She was frozen, mindless and breathless, a captive within her own fear.

"Your name," he prompted in a low, hard voice.

Somehow his speaking had let new air into the vacuum that had held her captive. The locked door in her mind swung open. "Bettina Bacheller," she croaked.

His face remained immovable, and she couldn't tell if he believed her or not.

"Hand that over," he demanded, pointing the gun toward her purse. "Hurry up."

She swallowed hard and, with shaky fingers, held the purse out to him. He kept the automatic weapon in his right hand and reached for her bag with his left. Holding it partially under his arm, he was able to open it and rummage through it while still keeping the gun and a careful eye directed toward her.

62 *A Siren's Lure*

"Don't move," he warned, although she had not shifted an inch. Even if she had wanted to, she could not have stirred.

"No," she whispered fearfully, "I won't."

He pulled out her billfold and passport and threw the purse to the hard stone floor. She watched remotely as the expensive leather handbag hit the ground and skimmed over the rough stones.

Still keeping the gun on her, he flipped through the documents, stopping at her picture and comparing it with the woman before him. Same pale blond hair, same green eyes. The only difference was that the woman in the picture had a confident smile that seemed to say, "The world is mine to own," whereas the woman standing before him now was not smiling at all. Her mouth was tight with the fear he had seen a thousand times before, the fear he himself had felt on occasion—of not knowing whether one was going to live or die.

"In there," he said, swinging the gun toward an open room with a bank of windows that looked out upon the night. "On the couch."

She turned slowly and walked in front of him, aware of each footfall behind her on the stone floor. The room he indicated was not large, but it had an L-shaped white couch, a low, lacquered coffee table and the same terrazzo flooring as the entry. Three or four ficus trees grew in clay pots, and on every surface in smaller containers were the ubiquitous flowers of the island. The lighting was dim, with only one lamp on the table behind the couch giving a yellow glow to the furnishings. In the reflection of the window, she could see him behind her, dressed in a loose-fitting brown

A Siren's Lure 63

sweater and tan slacks, and she wondered, not for the first time in several minutes, if he was really the type of man who could kill her without a qualm.

She reached the couch and sat down, wiping the moisture from her hands on the wool of her cream-colored slacks. The nights were still very cool in Capri, so she had worn a lamb's-wool sweater. But the fear was so hot within her that she felt as if she were going to suffocate inside it.

She watched him sit on the longer section of the couch and place her billfold and passport on the table in front of him. Staring hard at her, he laid the pistol beside him on the couch. "If you move," he said, once again in that low, even voice, "I'll make you very sorry."

She shook her head, indicating that she wasn't about to move, but he didn't notice. He had pulled out a small knife from his pocket and was starting to lift the corner of her photograph from her passport.

"No!" she cried, finally able to dislodge the jammed-up fear inside her. "Please don't! I won't be able to get out of the country. There is no other picture under that one."

He lifted his eyes to her face, the knife poised at the corner of her passport photo, and he studied her for a long, uneasy moment.

"I really am who I say I am," she said, softly, tentatively, frightened of those deep, brown eyes that bore into her with relentless scrutiny.

After what seemed like an interminably long time, he folded the knife back up and dropped it onto the table, then leaned back against the couch and held the gun on her once more.

"Won't you put that away?" she asked, feeling much bolder now after her first successful attempt to sway him.

He just shook his head. "Not a chance, lady. You've got some questions to answer first." He crossed one ankle over the other knee. "Start talking," he prodded.

"I told you, I am Bettina Bacheller."

"Why are you here?"

"On the island?" She hesitated for only a second; then the old confident Bettina surfaced again. "Well, I've always heard it's so lovely and—"

The soft click of the slide pulled back on the automatic pistol was the next sound she heard, and it froze the words in her throat. The gun was no longer limp in his hand; it was held stiff and ready, aimed directly at her head.

She swallowed with difficulty and opened her mouth to speak, this time truthfully. "I'm here to see you," she said softly.

He didn't move, nor did his eyes flicker. It was as if he had known her reason all along.

"You don't seem surprised," she ventured.

"You've been showing my picture around the island," he stated evenly. "I want to know why."

"It was the only way I could find you."

"Why did you want to find me?" he asked, his voice so controlled, so tight.

"Because I need your help in locating my father. Could you please lower that gun?" she asked almost pitifully.

He didn't seem a bit moved by her supplication. His eyes narrowed and were watching her even more closely than before, studying her suspiciously. When he spoke, his mouth was cautious and restrained. "What makes you think I could locate anyone?"

She tried to hold his stare, but faltered as her eyes dropped to the gun. Forcefully, she lifted them back to his face. "Because you have a reputation for that sort of thing."

The pistol wavered slightly and then lowered to his knee; the gun was still aimed at her, but was not as imminently threatening. It was as if some vital fluid had leaked out of him, yet the effect was evident only in the hand that held the gun. The rest of his face and body was still sealed. He was being very careful in his silence, holding his expression and his thoughts in check. He chuckled, but it was a nervous laugh at best. "Who told you such a thing?"

She wasn't about to give Jerry's name. She had promised him that she would do nothing to reveal the trap. So she was forced to lie again, and she wondered how many lies she would have to pile on top of one another before she could convince this man to help her. "It was a long time ago. I knew some people in the government." She shrugged, looking directly at him, hoping her evasive use of the word "government" would be clear to him. "I heard your name."

A muscle snapped in his jaw as he stared at her. "You've got the wrong guy."

She shook her head slowly. "I don't think so."

"You said it was a long time ago. You could be mistaken."

66 *A Siren's Lure*

"I'm not."

He let out a slow breath and then took in a much deeper one. He had to know; he had to find out how much this woman actually knew about him. "John Stewart doesn't know anyone in the government," he said.

She regarded him for a long moment, examining the cool, inexpressive facade that masked what had to be a severe emotional turmoil at this moment. "No," she said slowly, "but Upton John Erickson does."

He stared at her, his eyes fixed, his expression unchanged except for the slight jump of the nerve in his jaw. He pushed himself off the couch and turned his back to her, easing the catch of the pistol back into place so that it would not fire accidentally. His fingers raked through his dark hair as he walked away from her toward the window. A three-quarter moon hung over the island, and the sea lay dark with mystery and unseen spirits below. After staring out for a long time, he finally spoke with his back to her. "No one knows I'm here."

She sighed, letting the momentary doubts about what she was doing to this man slide away. Right now, the most important thing was to find her father. If she lived through this ordeal, she would deal with her conscience later. "I do," she answered.

He spun around and glared at her, his brown eyes fueled by a dangerous fire. He began to stalk her, slowly, circuitously, like an animal who knew it was dominant and that, with one sharp blow, it could kill and devour its opponent. He moved around the far end of the couch and the table before stopping in front of her. Then he leaned down, one hand resting on the back of the couch, the other holding the point of the gun at her neck. Her pulse there began to pound. The metal tip was cold, and when she swallowed, the action burned a path down her throat and chest. His face was so close that she could smell the mixture of his cologne with her perfume. The shaft of the pistol slid slowly along the vein in her neck, dipping into the hollows of her throat, before gliding even lower to a spot just above her breast.

"You are a beautiful and very tempting woman," he murmured, his breath warm against her face. "I'll give you that. But I have done an uncounted number of dastardly deeds in my time. You might be just one more to add to the long list."

She stared up at him, her eyes fixed on his, her mouth still and tight. His voice held a menacing quality that could easily have sent her over the edge of fear. But it was his eyes that gave him away. The brown contacts covered and hid the true color of his eyes, but they could not hide the whole man beneath them. They could not disguise what was in his soul.

"I don't think so," she whispered, finding courage in those deep, earthy-colored eyes of his. "I really don't think so."

He stared at her while the unlimited number of options volleyed back and forth in his mind. He ought to put her out of his life right now. He ought to, but...

Erickson straightened up slowly, drawing the pistol away from her body and letting it hang limply at his side. He went back to the window and stood looking out toward the left, at the twinkling lights of villas that formed earthbound constellations across the sloping hills of the island.

"How did you find out I was here?" he asked, speaking to her reflection in the window.

Bettina shifted on the couch for the first time since she had sat down, and she observed his back from across the room. The shock was gone. Now there was only fatigue in the slope of his broad shoulders. "I told you, I have friends. Someone spotted you here a couple of years ago." He spun around, surprised, but she just shrugged. "They thought you had moved on," she explained.

"If that's true, then why did you look here?"

She ran her manicured hand along the back of the cotton fabric of the couch. "It was the only lead I had. I had to start somewhere."

He chuckled grimly. "Looks like you hit pay dirt, doesn't it?" He turned around and, sighing heavily, opened the French doors to the terrace. "I knew it would happen sooner or later," he mumbled, then stepped out onto the deck and rested his hands on the balcony railing.

Bettina stood up and forced calm back into her shaking knees and legs. She went out onto the patio and stood beside him, both of them silent as they surveyed the island and the night spread out like a starlit cloth above and below them.

The balcony was in line with the sheer drop of the cliff, and below it was a verdant plateau dotted with lamplights that burned dimly from the cottages among the moss and broom. There were orchards, too, but they appeared only as gray blotches between the lights.

A Siren's Lure 69

Beyond the plateau, Bettina could see nothing but the darkness of the sea. To the right, the coast of Sorrento was a brilliant crescent of light, a frenzied array of nightlife that contrasted sharply with the peace and serenity that isolated this island from the rest of the world's chaos. The trill of a nightingale wove through the orchard at the side of the patio, its song sweet and clear in the cool jasmine-and-orange-scented air.

"So what are you going to do with this knowledge you have of me?" he asked, his voice rough and cold beside her.

She continued to gaze out over the cliff. She was so far from home, so far away from all that was familiar. She was in a place she had never been before. She had confronted a man who had spent five long years building a life that would hide him from all confrontations in that other world. And now she was standing on his patio, the jagged spikes of the cliff so close, so sharp, so dangerous. But it was precisely because she had come so far and wanted this so badly that she would not back down now. Not out of fear, anyway. From this point on, there was no turning back.

She turned and leaned her side against the railing so that she could face him. He was looking down at her, waiting for her answer, so she provided it. "I will do nothing," she replied in a steady, assertive voice. "Nothing...if you help me out."

Erickson regarded her face in the moonlight. It was a face that reflected her confidence, very beautiful and cool, without a lot of sentimentality. His kind of woman. And yet, he didn't think he liked this one much. Taking in the soft, furry green of her sweater, a color that matched her eyes perfectly, and the long length of her legs covered by cream slacks, he knew that he was attracted to her in ways that he wished he were not. Yet he was truthful enough with himself to realize that if anyone were seduced here tonight, it would probably be he.

But he didn't like her. She had ripped the rug out from under him, and he didn't trust her not to yank the whole floor next. His private life, the one he had struggled so hard to create for himself, was now shattered. And if this woman knew where he was, who else might know? Had the agency known all along and was it just waiting for the perfect moment to throw the net over him? Had she been sent to do it? He had never felt totally secure with his new image, so he had never grown complacent. He had always been a cautious man, thorough and meticulous with details. No, he had never grown complacent. But he had developed a sense of freedom in the past year that had given him room to play and to forget, if only for a few short hours here and there. But no more.

His eyes followed Bettina's to the table on the terrace. She looked back at him, her green eyes curious and wide. She hadn't noticed the table when she had first come on the deck, and now she was surprised to see it set with fine silver and crystal. A coral hibiscus lay on top of one of the plates. "You planned dinner for me after all?"

"I didn't know for sure what I would learn about you," he answered truthfully.

She paused. "And now?"

A Siren's Lure 71

Erickson glanced at the table and then back at her. Without answering, he walked over and lit the candles in the center. He picked up the bottle of Vernaccia and popped the cork. After pouring two glasses full, he held one out to her.

She stared at his mouth. He wasn't smiling exactly, but he had relaxed his lips to the point where the slightest movement could turn them into a smile. Had he resigned himself to his fate, or did he have an alternate plan up his sleeve?

She stepped over and took the glass from him. Her fear had blocked out most of the sensations of this house and this night; just as she had not noticed the table or the scent of jasmine until only moments ago, she now became aware that soft music played on a tape machine inside the door.

"Is that from *La Bohème*?" she asked, taking a sip of the delicious nectar-flavored wine.

"Yes. Do you understand Italian?"

"Only enough to get by when I have to. I understand that she is singing something about being called Mimi, but her name is Lucia. What else is she saying?"

Erickson listened for a moment, then translated. "'I live alone, quite alone, there in a little white room. I overlook roofs and sky. But when the thaw comes, the first sunshine is mine, April's first kiss is mine!'" He paused. "There's no more I can tell you about myself," he said, and Bettina wondered if he was still translating or if he was now speaking about himself.

"That's lovely," she said.

72   *A Siren's Lure*

Erickson pulled out a chair for her, and she sat down. He leaned close to her face once more. "I don't suppose—if I go into the kitchen to get the food—I don't suppose there is a chance that you'll be gone when I get back or that this will have been a dream."

Bettina felt her body catapult from the texture of his voice so warm against her cheek, and she smiled up into his steady brown eyes. "Not a chance."

He nodded slowly in acceptance. "I didn't think so."

After he had gone through the French doors and into the house, Bettina sat back in her chair and took several deep, relaxing breaths, her first since coming to his house. The evening breeze wafted around her, swirling all of the heady fragrances of the island into an intoxicating blend of orange and lemon and jasmine. The blinking of lights from the trattorias and cottages below were like the flickering of tiny candles between the locust trees and ferns.

She thought about what she had done tonight, but the memory of Erickson's threatening response rattled her nerves even as it filled her with a new thrill of confidence and power. She tried to think of him as nothing more than a man who had been caught in his own game, as a soldier and an agent for the government whose time it was finally to come in out of the cold. But most importantly, she tried to think of him only as the justifiable means to her own ends. She did not want to think of him as a man who had been running scared for five years. She did not want to picture his peaceful life among the flowers, the vineyards and the blue-green grottos. She did not want to hear in her

A Siren's Lure 73

mind the warmth of his voice or see in his eyes the depth of the earth. But despite her faithfulness to her own goals and her deep desire to find her father, she could not stop the images of Erickson that kept coming to her.

Her conscience was relieved from further self-analysis when he returned with a generous plate of *prosciutto con melone*, a loaf of crusty bread, a dish of *pasta mista* and a steaming bowl of prawns.

"You must like living here very much," she remarked, after he had served her plate.

"Yes," he said, gazing out over the cliff. "It suits me perfectly. I've gotten to know the island quite well. I climb and hike and scuba-dive."

"You were a SEAL with the navy, weren't you?"

He glanced at her, surprised and suspicious again. "Yes," he answered, still not trusting her enough to say more than was necessary.

"I don't know too much about the SEALs, other than the fact that their training is supposed to be so tough it makes the Green Berets look like overnight cub scouts."

He laughed at that, a deep, rich sound that poured through her like the fine, mellow wine they were drinking. "Yeah, BUDs—that's what we call the basic training—it was pretty tough."

"Actually," she said in a slow, almost questioning voice, "I've been doing some reading about the SEALs, and…they were referred to as America's most efficient assassins."

His fork stopped in midair and his eyes caught with hers. But it took him only a moment to recover.

A Siren's Lure

"Typical recruiting literature." He chuckled lightly, trying to brush it off.

But she couldn't let it go. She had to know. "Would you have killed me earlier if I hadn't answered your questions satisfactorily?"

He set his fork down and picked up his wineglass, taking a drink as he watched her over the rim. "You didn't answer them satisfactorily."

"So why haven't you killed me?"

"I need answers."

She nodded slowly and swallowed. "I see."

He couldn't look away. She kept those green eyes of hers trained on him until he wanted to slither off and hide under a rock. "Look, I didn't harm you, Miss Bacheller."

"But you might."

"I might not."

Her heart was racing a mile a minute, and she didn't know why she was so obsessed with having the perfect answer to that question. He was right, in a way. He hadn't killed her or even harmed her, and that should be all that mattered.

"I don't even know what to call you. Do I call you Erickson or Stewart or…or John?"

"John would be nice."

They ate in silence for a few minutes.

"This is delicious," she said. "Did they teach you how to cook like this in—what is it called? Buds?"

"Yeah, BUDs." His smile was faintly amused. "And no, they didn't spend too much time on gourmet-cooking classes. Most of the time we were eating mud."

A Siren's Lure 75

"I remember eating mud pies when I was little. They weren't so bad."

His eyes were tolerant and much older than hers at that moment. "Bettina," he mused. "That's an unusual name."

"It was my grandmother's."

He leaned his elbows on the table and clasped his hands, his eyes narrowing on her face. "Something tells me that Bettina Bacheller is all alone in the world. Am I right about that?"

She took a quick drink of wine. "Are you trying to find out who would miss me if you tossed me over the cliff?"

He smiled at that. "I'm not planning on tossing you over any cliff."

"Maybe you were thinking of burying me in the orange grove, then."

He laughed again and sat back in his chair, crossing an ankle over one knee. "You have a very active imagination."

"Not so imaginative, considering tonight's events."

He just shrugged and poured them both another glass of wine. "So," he said when he had relaxed in his chair once more, "suppose you tell me about the father you want me to find. What is his name?"

"Stephen Bacheller."

"And from the looks of his daughter, a very wealthy man, I presume."

"He was in the import-export business," Bettina said by way of explanation.

"Was?"

76 *A Siren's Lure*

"He died seven years ago." His confused look made her add hurriedly. "Or at least I thought he had died. But apparently, he hasn't."

"What happened to him?"

"Nothing...yet."

"He's not missing?"

"Not really."

John shook his head and frowned. "I'm lost, Miss Bacheller. If he's not missing and nothing's happened to him, why do you think he needs to be found?"

She ran her fingers up the stem and around the rim of her wineglass, studying the pale color of the wine in the light of the candles. "He goes by another name," she replied hesitantly, then looked up at Erickson. "Le Chat Noir."

Erickson choked on his wine and quickly set the glass down on the table, staring at her in disbelief. "Le Chat Noir! You are joking!"

"I see you've heard the name before," she answered grimly.

His eyes still held the same spark of amazement. "Your father is Le Chat Noir!"

Bettina's mouth remained tight in embarrassment and disgust over this whole matter. How could her father have done this to her! How could he! "You act as if he's some sort of celebrity," she remarked with disdain.

"Well, he is," John said, still notably impressed.

Bettina lifted her chin. Her eyes swept arrogantly over his face. "What, pray tell, is so wonderful about a thief?"

A Siren's Lure 77

"He's a master. And believe me, I ought to know."

"Oh?" She tilted her head as she looked at him. "Why is that?"

He leaned forward, his elbows resting on the table, his eyes boring into her lofty facade. "Because I'm a master," he said very softly, very intimately.

She picked up her wineglass and held it in front of her mouth, just touching her lips. "At what?"

His smile was slow and lazy as his eyes seemed to stroke every inch of her face. "At entering enclosed premises without an invitation, for one thing."

She tried to break the intimacy of the moment by taking a sip from her glass and gazing out to the coast on the horizon. "Can you find him?"

He shrugged and relaxed back in his chair. "Maybe. What's in it for me?"

She folded her hands in her lap and regarded him with a cool, bold expression. "A finder's fee."

"I don't need your money," he said, keeping his eyes fastened on her.

"And," she added, still regarding him closely, "your freedom."

Erickson took a drink of his wine to calm the sudden racing of his pulse. There were always ways out of unfriendly situations. But for now, he'd play along and see what happened. "Le Chat Noir has eluded capture so far," he pointed out.

"But," she coaxed, "as you admitted, you're a master."

He stood up and went over to the railing. There was always a way out. Always. "I'll have to sleep on it," he said.

Bettina sat quite still for a minute and then laughed out loud. She rose and joined him at the edge of the balcony. "And I suppose this is where I'm supposed to say, 'Okay, Mr. Stewart, you sleep on it and let me know tomorrow.'"

He turned toward her and smiled.

She shook her head. "Sorry, but I'm not that naive. If I leave you tonight, what's to keep you from packing up and taking off to—Madagascar or somewhere?"

He regarded her with his own thoughtful expression. "Madagascar, huh? Not a bad idea." After a moment, his eyes narrowed in deliberate scrutiny of her. "Are you saying you don't trust me, Miss Bacheller?"

"Not for a minute, Mr. John Stewart Erickson."

With his elbow resting on the rail, he angled toward her, still smiling. "And what makes you think I wouldn't be able to escape you anytime I wanted?"

Trying to counter his intimidation of her, she leaned close to him, their faces now only inches apart. "Because then," she whispered, "you would not only have every branch of the military intelligence community after you, you would also have Bettina Bacheller after you."

He clicked his tongue against his teeth. "A most frightening but also intriguing idea." He reached for a coil of her hair and twirled it around his finger. "That could make for some wonderfully exotic fantasies, you know."

She smiled, trying not to melt from the feel of his hand in her hair.

A Siren's Lure 79

"So you're not leaving?" he asked in that same low, inviting tone.

She cleared her throat. "No."

"You're sleeping here with me, then," he stated, his fingers slipping to the hair at the nape of her neck.

"I'll take the couch," she proposed, hoping she sounded more emphatic than she felt at this moment.

"No need for that, Bettina. I have a big, firm bed."

Electric impulses were dancing inside her body, and she tried once again to shut off the current. It was the wine—surely that was what it was. She'd had too much of it, as usual. She had never learned her limit. And now this man, who smelled of the orange and lemon groves around him, and whose eyes were like the hungry, savage earth, was filling her with the most intoxicating, compelling desires she'd had in a long while. At the same time, she didn't trust this John Stewart with the falsely colored hair and eyes for one minute. He was a master at a lot of things—one of them, no doubt, seduction. But Bettina Bacheller had always been in control of her life. She had always called the shots, made the first moves, written the rules. And no island song was going to lure her into this man's arms. Not tonight, anyway. Not until she had exactly what she wanted.

She raised her chin and looked directly up at him, her eyes veiled with the barrier she had chosen to erect between them. "I'll take the couch," she said, and her voice, though soft and sweet, held a clear-edged tone of determination that no one—not even a man who had helped topple powerful governments—could sway.

Chapter Seven

The cigarette was held between his thumb and forefinger, and both hands were resting high against the window frame. The room behind him was in character with the rest of his house and with most of the houses on the island. The floor was bare wood, polished to a high gloss by a local woman who came in twice a week to clean. The double bed was an old four-poster, covered with a white cotton quilt. A small, white oak table sat next to it, and a matching four-drawer dresser was against the far wall. The two windows in the room were curtainless and open to the elements. No one lived nearby, so Erickson had all the privacy he needed.

The windows were open now because, even though it was cold, he wanted the fresh smells of the sea air and the orchards to fill the room. How many times in the past two and a half years had he stood and looked out upon those glittering lights, breathed in those same exotic smells, and tasted the same blend of loneliness and freedom that he did now? Sometimes it seemed as if he had been here forever. At other times, the past was so near, he could almost reach out and touch it.

A Siren's Lure

From deep within his memory, he could still hear Major Winston's laugh. "We don't need to worry about Captain Erickson anymore. It's all been taken care of. He's a traitor, you know." The incident always came back to him in quick flashes of memory, bits and pieces here and there, never as a whole: the antique chifforobe that he had hidden behind; the sound of a classical guitar; Winston's laugh, and then the clink of wineglasses in a toast; the explosion, the charred bodies, the identification that had saved his life, the jewels that gave him monetary freedom. Afterward, there had been a host of cities, so many he had passed through that he couldn't even remember all their names, and the times when fear had gripped him so tightly that the sweat in his body had seemed to congeal. There had been the anxious moments when he had almost been caught, the constant tails by ambitious agents, the endless looking over his shoulder.

And then he had landed on Capri. Coming here had been a risk; there weren't enough outlets from the island, and he could easily have been trapped. But he wasn't, and it had worked. He had bought this secluded house from an Italian writer and had firmly established himself as John Stewart, free-lance consultant and sometime recluse.

The end of the cigarette glowed red as he took a long draw and let the ashes fall to the floor unnoticed. Everything had worked fairly well until Bettina Bacheller came along. He was realistic enough to know that nothing could last forever; but still, it was hard to face the end. He liked the peace and solitude of this place, the endless winding pathways that led from the villages to the sea, the rocky cliffs gouged by ravines and

82   *A Siren's Lure*

grottoes, and the brilliance of the flowers beneath the almost always clear blue sky. He would miss Capri but he would have to move on. This was to be his life; he had made it so on that night five years ago. He had created his own fate, and now he was destined to make the most of it. He would not look back.

With his forefinger wrapped over the tail end of the cigarette, he took a last draw and stubbed it out in the ashtray on top of the dresser. He thought of the woman who was lying on his couch right now, the one who'd had the gall to ask him if she could borrow a shirt to sleep in. He exhaled slowly as images of her expanded inside him. He skin and hair and catlike eyes were an inflaming intoxicant to his already stimulated hormones. It had been a long time since he had been with an American woman, and until now, he hadn't thought that he missed them very much. The Mediterranean women he had known were warmer, darker, full of hot, sexual energy. But it would be nice to touch skin like Bettina's to let the heat of passion build a little more slowly and carefully.

He took a deep breath of salt sea air and tried to still the racing of his pulse. She was dangerous. He mustn't forget that. She was the one who had come here and shattered what little security he had been able to piece together.

Of course, the idea of tracking down Le Chat Noir did have an intriguing lure of its own. At times, John missed the challenge, the conflict, the constant pumping of adrenaline when he was on an assignment. The thought of tracing that crafty thief across the Continent was an amusing one. But he wasn't sure what to do with the old man's daughter. He didn't

A Siren's Lure 83

trust her at all, and he knew he should get away from her, go somewhere else and maybe start all over. Finding Le Chat Noir might not be worth the risk of getting himself caught and caged by the overpowering falconer he had been escaping for so long.

BETTINA OPENED HER EYES and saw him moving quietly across the terrazzo floor. It was still very early in the morning; only a slim ribbon of sunlight curved over the mainland in the distance. Erickson was dressed in army-fatigue-colored pants, a bulky sweater and hiking boots, and he held a small backpack in his hand.

"And just where do you think you are going?"

He turned around, and his gaze skimmed over the bare length of her leg thrown over the top of the blanket. He forced his eyes to her face. "You're awake. How was the couch?"

"Fine. Where are you going?"

His mouth curved sideways into a half smile. "You don't trust me, do you?"

"Just curious."

"Uh-huh. Well, if you must know, I thought I'd hike down the mountain for a swim."

She sat up against the end of the couch, the blanket bunched around her waist. She was wearing his large, beige T-shirt, which now hung off one shoulder. Fluffing up her hair with her fingers, she regarded him lazily from across the room. "What's in the pack?"

He glanced down at the haversack in his hand, then back at her. "Didn't anyone ever tell you about what happens to young ladies who poke their noses in places where they don't belong?"

84 *A Siren's Lure*

Bettina lifted her arms above her head in a lazy, catlike stretch. "I never listened."

"Obviously. But again, if you feel you must know every intimate detail of my life, this is my breakfast. Let's see, I have a hunk of *caciotta romana* cheese, a few slices of Parma smoked ham, a loaf of wonderful crusty bread, a jar of freshly squeezed orange juice and a flask of coffee."

She stopped stretching and stared at him. "Ooh, that sounds wonderful! I don't suppose—You won't mind if I tag along, will you?"

He leaned back against the wall, laughing. "Do you want to go because you're hungry or because you think I'm going to make a break for it, maybe swim to Naples or something?"

"That had entered my mind," she countered. "After all, you are a SEAL. You could probably do it with your ankles and wrists tied. So..." She tossed back the blanket and stood up. "I think I'll just come along with you."

His eyes swept down the length of her, standing across the room with nothing on but his shirt, which hung to the middle of her thighs and fell over her bare shoulder. Oblivious to the thoughts that were pouring like lusty red wine through his bloodstream at this moment, she hitched the shirt back up over her shoulder, but then it hung provocatively low in front.

"Do you have any idea how far down the water is?" he asked, trying to get his mind on track.

"I can handle it," she answered confidently.

"Dressed like that?"

She took in his appearance again. "I don't suppose you have something I could wear?"

A Siren's Lure   85

He observed her supremely confident expression for a moment. "You didn't come very prepared for this mission of blackmail, did you?"

"I didn't realize we were going to be traipsing over the countryside," she retorted. "All of my clothes are back at the hotel."

He contemplated this woman before him for a long moment, his mouth taking on the harsh line of a scowl. "Did you ever *not* get anything you wanted, Miss Bacheller?"

She padded barefoot across the cool floor, stopping just in front of him, and lifted her chin up as she examined his expression and his question. Finally, she smiled and answered, "Never."

THE WHITE-HAIRED MAN, dressed in an impeccably tailored, dove-gray suit, sat forward in the straight wooden chair and rested his hands on the top of his gold-handled cane. His eyes were trained on the much older, hunchbacked man who was leaning over the table a few feet away. There was a bare light bulb above the table, hanging down from the ceiling by its wire. Two magnifying glasses of different intensities were on the table, a third was in the old man's hands. Newspaper was spread out across the table, and on top of it was the mosaic.

The hunchback crumpled into his chair and dropped the magnifying glass, his eyes closed and his head hung low.

"I am sorry, Vittorio," the white-haired man said. "You are tired."

"I am old, that is all."

"I could trust no one else with this."

86   *A Siren's Lure*

"I know." After a minute, the old man lifted his head and stared at Stephen Bacheller. "And yes, it is Byzantine."

Bacheller stood up and walked over to the table, picking up the framed mosaic of the Annunciation. It was intricately inlaid with cubes of glass that had been fused with gold, and with pieces of precious stones depicting the winged angel before the throne of the Madonna.

"Artists under the Comnenian dynasty often signed their names to their work. See here." Vittorio pointed to the scratching in the lower left-hand corner.

"But did it belong to Monreale?"

"After Good William had the cathedral built there, he buried many treasures beneath the cloister—or so it is believed. He was a true Norman, and although he continually challenged the Moslem supremacy, he must have thought there was a chance that much of the cathedral could be destroyed." Vittorio shrugged. "Many things were also found buried under the royal palace there."

Stephen held the mosaic up to the light. "And this? Was it one of those pieces?"

The old man nodded slowly. "It was stolen from the cathedral around 1890 and apparently passed from a Russian aristrocrat to a Turkish family and then somehow filtered down to Giuseppe Ruocco of Firenze." He stared pointedly at Stephen. "Now it has passed to you."

Bacheller lowered the mosaic and held it carefully in his hands. "It won't be with me long."

"It is authentic and is worth a fortune. But I do not know how you can possibly sell it."

A Siren's Lure 87

Stephen laid a hand on the old man's shoulder. "Not to worry, my friend. I already have."

THE CLIFFS surrounding them were wild and craggy. Rough, jagged walls dropped sharply to the sea, and the footpaths were steep.

"Getting tired?" Erickson asked after they had gone quite a way down the hill.

"No, no," Bettina hurried to assure him. "I love to walk." But as soon as he turned his back and continued down the narrow pathway, her shoulders sagged with the fatigue she refused to let him see. She had to stop and roll up the cuffs on the tan poplin pants he had lent her, and she retied the drawstring waist, cinching it tighter to keep the pants from sliding down. She was wearing the same T-shirt she had slept in, but she had tied it up in a knot at her waist. Erickson had offered her a pair of his shoes, but since he wore about a man's size twelve, she figured she would be better off in her own low-slung sandals. It was still chilly this early in the morning, and Bettina was glad she had taken his advice and worn a jacket. But, like his other clothes, it was much too large and cumbersome for her to feel comfortable in.

Few people were out at this hour. A young goatherd tended his flock, and a woman picked herbs from a field and laid them across a flat rock to dry. Even the birds seemed to be asleep. Only an occasional sea gull soared overhead, dipping and turning in the soft coral light.

Bettina watched Erickson move among the bushes and rocks with ease and dexterity. If she had not come along, would he have tried to escape her, she wondered. Or was he really going for an innocent swim, as he claimed he did every morning?

She paused and sat down on a large boulder to catch her breath. A moment later, either because he no longer heard her footfalls or because in some other way he sensed that she was not behind him, he stopped, turned around and walked back to her. With one foot propped up on a rock, he leaned down and rested an elbow on one knee. "How are you doing?" he asked.

"Wonderful," she gasped. "Can't you tell?"

He looked up at the hill down which they had climbed. The houses were left behind now; only the grottoes and ravines were still ahead. The sound of cool water trickling over the stones from an inland stream was the only noise that reached their ears.

He chuckled at her tired expression and grasped her hand. "Come on, we don't have much farther to go."

"What do you consider far?" she asked and got another laugh from him in response. But she kept her hand in his, marveling at how large and strong it was as he led her down over the crib moss and along the path that was carved into the rock.

"Since you feel the need to glue yourself to me today," he said with a smile, "you might as well tell me everything you can about your father."

She noted the smile and wondered if he was merely being crafty, perhaps hoping to catch her with her guard down so that he could either throw her over the cliff or get away from her. If that was the case, she wasn't about to fall for it. Since she was not above turning this man in to the authorities, she certainly

A Siren's Lure 89

wouldn't allow his charm to make her lose her head—not even for a second.

"What do you want to know?"

"I want to know everything you can remember about him. Little characteristics, habits, his work, everything."

"Well," she said, taking a deep breath. She had let go of his hand now that they were on more of a straightaway. The track was following the gentle slope of a vineyard, and it appeared to be another quarter of a mile before they would reach the final cliff that would bring them down to the water. "I guess I'll start with his business. He was, as I told you before, in the import-export trade."

"What kinds of things did he import?"

"Oh, rugs, antiques, cars, jewels, paintings—you name it, he provided it. He traveled all over the world. He spent quite a bit of time in Europe, of course, and in Egypt and parts of Asia—mostly Japan and Thailand. He made a few trips to South America, especially Peru and Brazil."

"Did you ever go with him?"

"When I was younger and if it was summertime or a school break, he would take me. It was wonderful. We had such fun together." She was smiling to herself. "Daddy really knew how to put on a show for me. He took me to the best hotels, the flashiest shows and restaurants. He liked glitz and dazzle."

"From what I know of Le Chat Noir, that fits."

"Oh, yes, he was a colorful man, sort of swaggering and flamboyant. Never ostentatious, though; he had a lot of class."

90 *A Siren's Lure*

Erickson stole a glimpse of the woman walking beside him, one of the classiest women he had met in a long time. "Yes, I imagine he did. What about your mother?"

"She died when I was very young. I hardly remember her."

"How did it happen?"

"Leukemia."

"You had no brothers or sisters."

"No."

"It must have been lonely when your father left you and went away on all those trips."

Bettina fixed her eyes on the path ahead. "He always brought me wonderful things, and we spent time together when he was home."

"Still, for a young girl...Who took care of you when he was gone?"

She shrugged. "We had a series of housekeepers and such who hung around. I had company if I wanted it."

"I see." Erickson's voice held all the dispassion his military training had taught him, revealing nothing of the thoughts that hovered between the words. "What memories do you have of your mother?"

Bettina glanced over at him, perturbed. "Is this really necessary?"

"It could be. I want to know everything I can about your father, and knowledge of the woman he married could tell me something about him."

She sighed. "My memories are fairly sketchy. I remember soft things, you know, like touches and a voice and a laugh...although they may not be memories as much as some childish fantasy I cooked up."

A Siren's Lure 91

"Did he ever talk about his relationship with her?"

The path began to narrow again as they neared the edge of the cliff. Sea gulls were carried on the eddies of air, and the murmur of the surf soared along the currents of the salty sea breeze. "No, not really. Occasionally I would go into the library and catch him holding her picture in his hands, just staring down at it, somber-like."

She stopped as a thought came to her, and Erickson paused in the track beside her. Her voice became soft and tentative, and he had to strain to hear it over the screech of the gulls. "Once, when he didn't know I was standing there, I saw him run his finger across the picture—in what I would call a loving way. He looked so very, very sad."

She looked up at Erickson with a bewildered expression. "I had forgotten all about that. Funny, isn't it, the things you remember when..." The thought trailed away with the memory, and she resumed walking, leaving it behind in the dust. "Whenever I was around, I felt that I was the only one who existed in his eyes. He made me feel that way."

"Did he ever talk to you about his business? Here, let me help you down. This is pretty treacherous."

She felt his big hands come up beneath her arms and beside her breasts, and he lifted her down to the goat track he had jumped onto. When he lowered her to the ground, the shirt she was wearing brushed against his chest. Although both of their bodies jolted with the awareness of the touch, neither paused to show it.

He went on ahead, holding her hand as they traversed the sharp wall covered with thick vegetation and helping her over the rougher spots. Presently, they

92   *A Siren's Lure*

reached a tiny cove with the sheer rock wall rising above and behind them. The water here was shaded by the colors of depth. In the shallow spots, it was a brilliant emerald; where it became deeper, it was blue; and where it dropped off to unknown depths, it was like lapis lazuli and indigo.

After they had settled themselves on large boulders at the water's edge, Erickson asked the same question again. "His business, did he talk to you about it?"

"Nothing that seems really important. He always told me about the people he met, the places he went, the wonderful things he saw and bought...at least I thought he had bought them. Maybe he stole everything all along—oh, I don't know!" She turned her head away and watched the morning light slide across the surface of the water. "It's funny how you think that you know a person, but then you learn that you didn't know him at all."

"And you're disappointed in what you've learned about him?"

She gaped at John. He had removed his pack and jacket and was leaning back on his elbows. "Well, of course I am! Who wouldn't be?"

"Maybe you had unrealistic expectations of him. Maybe he was never what you thought he was."

She looked down and fingered the bottom of the nylon jacket she was wearing. "I thought my father hung the moon."

Erickson studied her expression, but held back any empathy he might have had for her. "When was the last time you saw him?"

"Seven years ago. He was going to Kenya with some friends and from there to Nepal. I wanted to go, but

A Siren's Lure 93

for some reason, he didn't want me along on that trip. I didn't understand why, but I tried to push it out of my mind. I was busy with friends anyway. It was early spring, and the—the social season was getting under way.''

"Social season. You say that as if it's a dirty word.''

"Well, you know, after a while, it started getting stale. It was the same old thing night after night. Oh, one night I'd be on a yacht and the next night at someone's summer home on the Cape, but essentially it was the same people with the same old lines.''

"How did you learn of his death?'' John asked, not yet ready to delve too deeply into her personal life.

"I didn't, until the men he had gone with came home. He had told them to go on without him, but the problem was he never came back. When I contacted the authorities in Nepal, they informed me that he had taken a pack trip up into the Himalayas and had somehow fallen off a ridge to his death. His body was never found in the snow.''

Erickson observed her sitting there so solemnly, so still. One minute she was like a lost little girl, and the next minute she was like a rock. How to deal with a woman's delicate emotions was one thing the navy hadn't trained him to do, and he was now at a loss. "Hey, how about a swim?'' he asked.

"What did you bring to swim in?''

His smile was mischievous. "I come to this cove because no one else does. It's very secluded and private.''

She pursed her lips. "Don't look at me as if you can't wait to see my shock and dismay. I've gone skinny-dipping before.''

94 *A Siren's Lure*

"I'm sure you have." He waited for a moment, watching her. "Well?"

"Well what?"

"Are you going to go in or not?"

Her eyes swept across the horizon, where the indigo-blue of the sea met the pale greenish blue of the morning sky. "Do you mind if I swim in your shirt?"

"Not at all. Would it make you feel better if I wore something?"

She considered the strong male body beneath his clothing, then released a quick, laughing sigh. "Yes."

It was a game, she knew that. And these were merely rules that they were setting up and guidelines to follow. She had played the game many times before, but somehow it had never seemed quite so serious. Always before, it had been more coquettish, more flirtatious. Here, she was setting up rules because she really wanted a barrier between them. She didn't want to get too close to this man or feel too much. She would play the vamp if that was what it took to get what she wanted from him. But she was not going to play that role for keeps.

She removed the jacket and the drawstring pants he had lent her. The T-shirt was long and covered her as much as a short dress might. His own T-shirt was shorter, but he wore some drab green GI-issue boxer shorts that could, if she didn't know the difference, be taken for swim trunks.

There was no beach, only rocks that dropped off into the emerald water. He jumped in first and then, with his hands under her arms, eased her down in front of him.

A Siren's Lure   95

"Brrr!" she squealed. "I didn't realize it would be so cold!"

He laughed. "You'll get used to it after a while. Come on, get in deeper and start swimming." He let go of her and dove under the water, swimming beneath the surface for about twenty-five feet. He came up in a deeper, bluer part.

"Oh, you must be crazy, Bettina!" she cried to herself as she followed his lead and dove beneath the water. She surfaced after about five feet, shivering and squealing from the cold. He laughed and sent a wave of water splashing over her, then dove under once again. She treaded water for several minutes and floated on her back, while he swam like a fish a long way out.

Eventually he came back, and they raced each other toward the rocks. Laughing, she tried to climb out of the water, but he had to help her up onto the stones. With his hands on her sides, lifting her, the T-shirt rose above her thighs and their bodies touched, wet and clinging to each other. He held her that way, not lifting or lowering her, just holding her still in front of him for a long, electrifying moment. Then finally, in a blend of laughter and plea, she whispered, "Please, John, help me out."

Her T-shirt clung to her skin as they crawled up on the rocks. He couldn't take his eyes off her. She was not wearing a bra, and the outline of her body, with every curve and mound and hollow, was clearly visible.

She knew he was watching her, so she reached for the jacket to put it on. "It's cold," she said, knowing it sounded like a pretty feeble excuse, even though it was true. While he began to pull the food out of the pack, she ran her eyes over him. He was so lean and strong, and the wet shorts hugged his body in a most revealing way. He laid the food out on a flat rock, then opened the jar of orange juice and held it out to her.

She took the first drink and handed back the jar. He broke off a hunk of bread, put slices of cheese and ham on it, and gave her the food. Then he prepared the same for himself.

"This tastes wonderful," she said, pushing back her streaming-wet hair. "Do you do this often?"

"Every day."

"Really? Every morning you come down here to swim and eat breakfast?"

He took a bite of food and nodded. "Gets the blood pumping."

She laughed. "It does do that!"

His gaze swept hungrily down her body as he thought that swimming wasn't the only thing that got the blood pumping.

Bettina finished her meal and pulled her legs up, hugging her knees for warmth. "What do you do all day, John?"

"Different things. Why?"

"I just wondered. You live here alone, so secluded. I was just trying to picture your typical day. You said you consulted on international business. Was that true?"

"Yes. I do that some. I go over to Naples quite a bit and to Castellammare—all along the coast, really."

"I don't understand what you consult about."

His face was thoughtful and still, as if he weren't sure whether he wanted to talk about it. Finally, he shrugged and told her. "Basically, I work with companies that are doing business in war-torn countries or in countries where the leadership is very unstable. I work with the employees who will be traveling there and teach them how to...to survive. How to be a hostage, how to find routes out of a country, how to negotiate one's way out of certain situations."

She regarded him for a long moment, wondering how many times he had dealt with those situations on a personal basis. "Were you ever a hostage or a prisoner of war?"

He was quiet as he fixed those steady brown eyes on her. "I don't talk about the past."

"Why not?"

"Because it'd dead and gone. There's no point in it."

In a flash of insight that surprised her as much as him, she said, "The past is never dead. It's all there, waiting for you to remember and deal with it."

"The present is what matters now," he argued. "For you, that means finding your father. For me, it means doing whatever I have to do to stay free." His voice grew cold and bland. "And you've made sure that includes helping you."

She didn't like his tone and she didn't want to do anything to press the issue with him. He was going to help her—that was good enough for now. "Could I have some of that coffee?"

With that same stony countenance, he reached for the thermos and handed it to her unopened, letting her fend for herself this time.

"Would you tell me what you've heard about Le Chat Noir?" she ventured, leaning back into the hol-

98 *A Siren's Lure*

low of the rock. The sun was higher now, and she could see the light on the water moving their way. In a few minutes, the rocks would be bathed in sunlight and warmth.

Erickson finally relaxed his own body and leaned back on his elbows. "He struck in Milan last week."

Her eyes widened in surprise. "How do you know that?"

"I keep up with him." John noticed her curious expression and decided to explain himself. "It's sort of a hobby of mine. I like to chart successful criminals' moves, to try to figure where they're going to strike next and what their systems are."

"Why are you so intrigued by them—and by my father in particular?"

He shrugged. "I guess because I used to do the same sort of thing. Only my jobs were all for the government. I enjoyed the work, and by following Le Chat Noir's moves, I can keep my mind active."

"And you think you can figure out his system when Interpol can't?"

He stole a glance at her expressive green eyes, then looked back toward the sea. "They don't know the mind of a criminal."

"And you do," she said softly.

His eyes caught with hers. "I do."

Bettina was the first to look away, and she shook her head in dismay. "I still can't believe it, though. My father, a criminal. Oh, how I hate the sound of that! I thought he was such a decent man..." She glanced quickly at Erickson and noted the tight line of his mouth. "I didn't mean—what I meant was·that I thought he was a law-abiding..."

A Siren's Lure   99

Erickson shrugged and kept his tone of voice expressionless. "Now you know."

She hurried to cover her tracks. "So where do you think he will go next?"

John narrowed his eyes in thought. "There are two possibilities. He's already hit twice in Italy. That points to the probability that he would move on to another country. At the same time, that's what Interpol would think, too. So the other possibility is that he'll stay here."

"But how will we know where he is in Italy?"

"Le Chat Noir has, like everyone else, a few idiosyncrasies. One of them is gambling. The other is enjoying the company of the very rich and famous." John debated with himself about how truthful to be with her. "One or both of these habits will eventually be his downfall."

Bettina was trying not to show any emotion, but it was reflected in the tight lips and unflinching eyes. "There are lots of cities that have casinos," she said, her voice as tightly controlled as her expression.

He watched her closely as he continued. "There is a festival every year at this time in Amalfi—at the close of the opera season. It's called the Festival of La Scala. Lots of international celebrities and very wealthy people come for the celebration. Le Chat Noir has been spotted at the opera—at La Scala, La Fenice and San Carlo. And from what I can tell about his movements, he never misses a festival anywhere."

"So you think he will go to Amalfi."

"If he stays in Italy, yes, I think he will go there."

Something glittered in her eyes, and she smiled at him. "You enjoy tracking his moves, don't you?"

100 *A Siren's Lure*

"I've got to keep my finger in the pie, even if it is only as a game, or I'll get rusty."

She laughed. "Well, we can't have that, now, can we?"

Erickson let his eyes linger on her for a long moment. Her hair was starting to dry, and she began fluffing it up with her fingers. The T-shirt had also dried, but she had not found the need to hurry and put on the pants. He liked that about her. She seemed fairly confident in her own body, not ashamed of it, while not inclined to flaunt it, either. It was the same with her looks. She knew she was beautiful but didn't seem to have a need to check her appearance constantly in the mirror or put on lipstick and eye makeup every five minutes. There was an easy, relaxed sexuality about her that he found appealing. The question was could he resist her? Or worse yet—did he want to?

"There is also a private gaming house in Amalfi that I feel sure that Le Chat Noir could not stay away from," he said, forcing the sexual thoughts of her to the back of his mind. "It's as good a place as any to start looking, especially since I have several contacts there."

Bettina cleared her throat and lifted her chin. "Then we'll leave the island in the morning?"

Erickson fixed his steady gaze on her and didn't move a muscle for what was to Bettina an agonizingly long time. "*We* are not leaving this island, my dear. *I* am leaving the island."

She kept her eyes riveted on his and her mouth tight, refusing to waver in the least.

"Oh, no, you don't," he said, shaking his head at her. "You can just get that look off your face right

A Siren's Lure   101

now. You might think you can tag along behind me for a swim or a walk around the island, but there is no way you are going with me on this.''

She retained the poker-faced expression with award-winning brilliance. ''This is my father we're talking about.''

''I work alone,'' he growled.

''I'm not about to let you catch up with him, only to have him take off again without seeing me.''

''I'll let him know that you are here.''

''I'm going with you, John.''

''No, you're not, lady.''

''I can help you.''

He chortled at that and let his gaze scan her with disdainful leisure. ''How can you help me?''

''I'm not totally useless, you know. I have a college degree. I also have a picture of my father that I always carry with me.''

He laughed out loud, and the sound echoed and bounced off the sculptured, rough-hewn cliffs. ''Well, by all means, then, if we need to impress anyone with your scholastic abilities, the degree will certainly come in handy. The photo might even be more enticing.''

''No need to be arrogant,'' she countered haughtily.

''Arrogant! Ha, that's a good one. You, my lovely young siren, wrote the book on arrogance. And the answer is still no. I work alone.''

There was silence in the air between them. When he glanced back at her, she had the same set expression, the same irrefutable confidence in herself, the same illogical and hardheaded conviction in her eyes. ''No, Bettina,'' he said again, and stood up to begin climbing down the rocks into the water. "You're not going to change my mind."

"Whatever you say...Erickson."

He stopped cold, his feet hanging over the rock as he readied himself to jump into the water. When he turned around, his eyes were glaring at her. "And you have the nerve to condemn your father for what he does," John said, his voice low and bitter. "You are no better, lady. You'll stoop to anything, won't you? You'll go to any lengths to get what you want. Well, I will not stand for blackmail. Do you understand me, woman? I won't stand for it. And you will not get away with it." He turned away and dove headlong into the water.

The sun had climbed higher in the sky, and the warm light now bathed the rocks in the cove. Bettina leaned back against the boulder she was sitting on, closed her eyes and smiled.

Chapter Eight

Alvin Bilgeworth's bulging stomach got in the way, but by shifting his weight a little to the left, he was able to pick the lock and get inside before the maid came out of the room next door and noticed him.

Once inside, he popped two antacid tablets into his mouth and chewed them up. All this Eye-talian garbage they called food over here made him want to puke. He belched as his eyes scanned the room. The bed was made and the bathroom was immaculate. It didn't look as if she'd been there last night at all.

He pulled back the cover and sheets on the bed, then drew them back up and neatly tucked them in. He opened the closet door and took out her vinyl-covered suitcase, tossing it on the bed. He flipped it open and rummaged through it. Some of her clothes were hanging in the closet, but she had left a lot of things in the bag. There were all these frilly underthings in every color—size five, but he already new that—a couple of nightgowns, shoes, stockings, a hair dryer, a curling iron, some shorts—size seven—and blouses—size eight.

104 *A Siren's Lure*

On the bottom of the suitcase, beneath all the clothes, was a manila envelope. Alvin slipped it out from the stack and opened it. Inside was her airline ticket, a Washington, D.C., phone number, a couple of pictures of two guys.... He stopped, held the pictures up side by side and studied them. One guy, with sandy-brown hair and blue eyes, was dressed in naval whites; the other guy, wearing some of those faggy Eye-talian shirts and pants, had much darker hair, brown eyes and a mustache. Alvin stared hard at both pictures, comparing the shape of the jaw and the height and weight of the bodies. There was something very similar about these guys. Maybe brothers...Maybe the same guy. He flipped the photographs over and saw the names on the backs. Erickson on one and John Stewart on the other.

He stuck the two pictures inside his Western-stitched polyester leisure suit, then slipped the manila envelope back under the clothes. After closing the suitcase and setting it down on the floor of the closet, he quickly fingered through the clothes hanging on the rod. There was a long beige knit dress that he would most assuredly like to see on that Bacheller gal. Sundresses, a jacket, slacks and some silk blouses made up the rest of the clothing. He plunged his pudgy fingers into the toes of her shoes on the floor to see if she had hidden anything there. Nothing.

He closed the closet door and checked the bathroom. Nothing there but toothbrush and toothpaste, a razor, some face goop and a hairbrush. When he came back into the room, he noticed a book lying on the dresser. *Il Sentiere al Nido d'Aragno*, by some joker named Italo Calvino. He flipped through it but

A Siren's Lure

couldn't read a word. Why these damned foreigners didn't learn English was beyond Alvin Bilgeworth.

He was about to set the book down when a piece of paper fell out of the center and fluttered to the ground. He bent over with a groan, his face flushed from the exertion and his breath labored, but he picked up the paper, holding it at arm's length to read what was written on it. "Caffè Solare—Punta Azzura." And scribbled beneath that was the name Erickson.

Alvin wasn't sure what it meant or what it might have to do with finding Stephen Bacheller, but at this point, any lead was worth checking out. He crammed the piece of paper into his pocket and left the room.

ERICKSON'S BEDROOM had suddenly been transformed into an ammunition depot.

"Are you planning on an invasion?" Bettina asked, standing safely back into the doorway.

The floor was littered with all kinds of military paraphernalia that he kept in a trunk buried under his closet. There were several different types of guns, a couple of knives, a shoulder harness for his pistol, flares, binoculars, spare clips, hand grenades and a bunch of other things that she'd never seen even in the movies.

"Just getting ready to go," he said without looking up. He picked through the pile, sorting and gathering exactly what he would need most. Those items he stuffed in a duffel bag, then placed the other equipment in the trunk and dropped it through the hole in the floor. He closed the trapdoor and stood up, holding a small silver pistol out to her. "You think you can carry this without shooting your foot off?"

106 *A Siren's Lure*

Bettina's resistance was instinctive. "No! Don't get that gruesome thing near me. I hate guns. You can protect me."

"I'm leaving the island, Bettina. Remember? I just thought you might want to keep this with you for protection."

"Why on earth would I want to do a silly thing like that?" She didn't wait for his reply, but twirled around and left the bedroom.

He stood still, the gun hanging loosely in his hand. She had something else up her sleeve, he could tell. But if she thought for one minute that she was going with him, she had a big surprise coming. No way would he let himself be strapped with a conniving female. That was absolutely, positively, out of the question.

"WORRIED SICK is what I've been, Bettina. How could you? You promised you would call!"

Bettina cringed at the furious tone in Jerry's voice. "I'm sorry; really I am. But after I confronted Erickson, I couldn't very well leave. He might have taken off, and then what would I have done?"

"Are you sure he didn't threaten you in any way?"

"I'm sure, Jerry." She hated to lie to him, but she could never tell him what had actually transpired last night. If he learned that Erickson had held her at gunpoint and threatened her life, he'd be on the next plane to Italy so fast, neither she nor John would know what hit them. No, it was better this way. What Jerry didn't know wouldn't hurt him, and since she had Erickson right where she wanted him, there was no point in throwing any other coals onto the fire.

A Siren's Lure 107

"I'm still worried, Bettina. I've been thinking about this a lot the past few days. I want you to back out. I'll help you find your father. You don't need to help me get Erickson."

"For heaven's sake, Jerry, I've come this far, so why should I back out now?"

"Because you don't know what Erickson will do, and I don't want you caught in any kind of cross fire down the line. He's capable of anything."

She knew she had to hang up before Jerry started making too much sense and before she started listening to it. "I'll call you from Amalfi," she promised. "So stop worrying. Things couldn't be going more smoothly."

THE ALISCAFO skimmed along the water, filled with passengers returning to Naples. A dozen soldiers sat in the back, making time with a group of girls who were on holiday. An old woman who was eating bread wrapped in a newspaper sat in front of them.

Bettina looked over at Erickson, who was stiff and glum beside her. "Don't be such a poor sport," she said. "You may find that you need me."

His sideways glance was disparaging, and he spoke softly out of the side of his mouth. "That'll be the day when I need help from some rich, spoiled female."

Her eyes dropped to the duffel bag between his feet, the bag that in her opinion held enough hardware to start World War III. She shuddered inwardly.

Erickson folded his arms across his chest and closed his eyes. With his sunglasses and loose-fitting pants and shirt, he looked very Italian. Bettina had noticed that he was careful not to speak English when anyone was nearby. It was all probably second nature to him; for years he had developed habits that would protect his identity and not bring any unwanted attention to him.

"Where do we get a car?" she asked, trying to keep her own voice low.

He opened his eyes slowly and, it seemed, with regret. "Would you know even if I told you?"

Her mouth tightened and her whisper had a hard edge to it. "I intend to be included in this, John. You are not going to shut me out."

He lifted the sunglasses and stared at her with disdain in those steady brown eyes. "Let me take care of the details," he said, and dropped the glasses back into place.

Bettina turned toward the window and sighed, telling herself it didn't matter. As long as he found her father, that was all she cared about. His bad attitude was his own problem, not hers.

He had already warned her before leaving Capri that she musn't talk about her father or about anything relating to what she and Erickson were doing unless they were sure they were alone. And since he had no desire to talk about himself, that left little in the way of conversational topics.

As the hydrofoil glided toward the Bay of Naples, Bettina focused her thoughts on what her father might be doing right now, where he was, whom he was with. She still couldn't put Stephen Bacheller together with Le Chat Noir. To her, they were separate people. One was the father she wanted to find; the other was the famous thief whom Erickson was planning to track down. John had said that once they got to Naples,

A Siren's Lure 109

they would rent a car and drive down the coast to Amalfi. The Festival of La Scala had begun that day, and since Erickson surmised that Le Chat Noir would go there, that was where they would go, too.

The *aliscafo* eased into the dock. Several passengers with their luggage stood up, hoping to be the first off the boat. Bettina glanced over at Erickson. His eyes were open now, and he was watching the mad exodus with a blank expression. Jerry was right again, of course; she didn't know what John would do. But she didn't think he would hurt her. If his intention was to get rid of her, he'd already had numerous chances to do it. She couldn't read much about this man in his eyes or in his face, but she could read enough to know that he wasn't a cold-blooded killer, efficient assassin or not.

THE AFTERNOON BREEZE filled the rental car as they drove along the bay toward the busy port of Castellammare di Stábia. A Puccini overture played on the radio, and in the backseat was a case of Tignanello, one of Erickson's favorite wines. If it weren't for all the military hardware in the trunk, and if Erickson would stop peering into the rearview mirror every two minutes, Bettina might be able to convince herself that she was on a carefree Italian holiday...with a devastatingly handsome Italian man.

She turned toward him and took a deep breath. "Do you mind if I ask you a question?"

He took his eyes off the road briefly to glance her way. "That depends."

"I was just wondering why you've been...hiding all these years." She knew what Jerry had told her, but

110   *A Siren's Lure*

she wanted to hear from Erickson what had really happened.

"I had my reasons."

"Obviously. I just wondered what they were. You've gone to fairly elaborate lengths not to be found."

"Not elaborate enough," he mumbled under his breath. "Which reminds me. You mentioned that you knew someone in the government. I assume by that you mean defense intelligence. Who is it?"

She looked quickly out the side window as they raced along the winding road. "I'm not at liberty to say," she said to the window.

He glanced over at her again and narrowed his eyes on her cool profile. "Why not?"

"It's...well, he's a personal friend of mine. And it's our secret."

"How personal a friend?"

She considered Erickson's question carefully. He had refused to disclose his past to her, so why should she lay out her whole life story to him? Let him wonder a bit, just as she was wondering about him. It would do him good. She focused her eyes on the road ahead and smiled. "Very personal."

"How does he know anything about me?" Erickson had his suspicions of who it could be. There were only four or five guys who had been on his case, any one of whom would gladly have made Bettina Bacheller a very personal friend.

"You're fishing, John."

He was quiet for a moment; then his voice came through roughly. "Is he here in Italy now?"

A Siren's Lure 111

Her expression was one of exasperation until she turned and saw him gazing fixedly into the rearview mirror. His face had hardened like a chunk of marble, and his eyebrows were drawn together in a dark scowl.

"I asked you if he was here," John growled.

"N-no. Of course not." She turned around in her seat and glanced behind them. There were several cars on the highway—a small red Fiat, a silver BMW, a couple of boxy little models she didn't recognize.

"Turn around," he commanded harshly. "Don't look back. Does your friend with the DIA know you're here? Does he?"

"No," she lied. If Erickson found out about Jerry, that would ruin everything. "No," she repeated, more emphatically this time.

"Then who knows you're here?"

"I—I don't know. I..." She sighed, then took in a deeper breath. "I had a little problem at home—before I left to come over here. It's possible that..."

He glowered at her before shifting his attention back to the road. "What kind of problem?"

"Well...it was with the IRS."

He frowned, waiting for a better explanation, so she plunged on.

"You see, I kept getting these crazy letters and warnings, saying that I owed this incredible amount of back taxes. It had nothing to do with me, really. It was revenue due on my father's estate. Apparently, he had—had not paid any taxes for quite a few years. And then, when evidence arose through Interpol that he might be this international jewel thief...well, they

112   *A Siren's Lure*

came down even harder on the estate. Everything was confiscated.

His eyes had turned to stone as he glared at her, but she didn't notice. She was wrapped up in the event and stared straight ahead.

"Everything I owned—except for a few personal items like clothes and my own jewelry. They took it all. It was a nightmare." She sighed, closing her eyes as she relived the horrible memory. "Everything was just...whisked away."

The road curved precipitously, passing caverns, inlets and bordering masses of orange and olive groves. The cliffs burgeoned with flowering trees and bushes as the car wound through tiny fishing villages. Suddenly Erickson pulled off onto a narrow side road that led down to a little harbor at the foot of the cliff. He switched off the engine and reached beneath his shirt into the shoulder harness for his gun. He jammed in a new magazine of cartridges, then leaned back against the seat and closed his eyes for a moment, ready and waiting for whoever would follow them down to the harbor. "Who is it?" he growled again.

"Who is—you mean following us?" Bettina stammered. "I have no idea, John. I really don't." Her own fear had taken hold, and with it came a new rush of anger. "But I wish you'd put that damn thing away. I'm sick of your waving it around in front of me. I'm sick of being afraid of you!"

He turned to her, his eyes narrowed to dark brown slits. His voice was low and hard. "And I'm sick of being afraid of you. I'm sick of worrying about the roadblock you may have waiting for me around the next curve. I'm sick of not knowing what kind of

A Siren's Lure   113

game you're playing with me." He grabbed her arm and yanked her closer; his husky voice was like sandpaper against her face. "You are playing a very deadly game, Bettina Bacheller. If I go down, you can bet your sweet life that you're going down with me."

As she stared into those hard brown depths of his eyes, she felt a fresh stab of fear. Where his hand was grasping her arm, it ached from the pressure he was exerting. "I'm not...please, I'm not playing a game. I'm—I'm looking for my father. Please..."

He worked hard to control his breathing and the racing of his heart. He listened for the sound of a BMW rolling down the lane behind them, but he heard nothing.

Erickson searched deeply into her eyes for truth, nearly losing himself somewhere in their cool, inviting depths. Glancing down at the arm he was clenching so tightly, John forced his fingers to relax, letting them slide back and forth against the blue cotton of her shirt sleeve. He lifted his hand and wrapped it around the back of her neck as he continued to stare at her, his pulse accelerating from a desire he did not want to feel. His gaze followed the planes of her face, seeking out the lies that he suspected were there but that he could not prove. She was so beautiful, she smelled so fresh, and her skin and hair were so pale, so lovely, so touchable.

But he must not forget for even a minute that she was here for one reason only—to find her father. She had already proved that she would do anything to get what she wanted. Erickson could accept that. For as long as it was just her father, he was safe. But what else did she want? What else was she hiding from him

114 *A Siren's Lure*

with those artful little smiles of hers? That was what bothered him.

He ran his calloused thumb across her smooth cheek, and she swallowed the new, strangling sensations. She was a mass of raw nerves, stretched thin and coiled tightly. The pressure of his thumb against her skin was hard and rough, yet without malice. He wasn't trying to hurt her, she knew that. But the restless power behind his hand, the intensity beneath his tightly controlled exterior, filled her with a frightening, exhilarating heat. He was capable of so much. Much more than he was showing. But what? Violence, to be sure, but she sensed that he also felt great tenderness and reckless masculine urges that he was having trouble holding at bay.

Her eyes dropped to the pistol, held loosely in his left hand. "No one's following us, John. Please put that away."

He drew back his hand, emptied the chamber and stuck the gun in the holster. "That BMW was."

"Maybe you're just being—well, you know..."

"Paranoid?" His mouth was now a harsh, thin line. She looked sheepish. "Well, yes."

"No." The answer was brusque. "I purposely made several wrong turns in Castellammare, but the BMW was always there, right behind us." He closed his eyes and pinched the bridge of his nose. "You have no idea what you've done to me. Dammit!" He slapped his hand against the steering wheel. "You come to me with the IRS and who knows who else on your tail. You lead them right to me."

"The IRS has no grief against you," she argued.

A Siren's Lure 115

His return glare was reproachful. "The military has a grief against me. I'm essentially AWOL. The United States government has a grief against me. I stole government property and took off. I have been accused of treason! And if I'm caught, I'll spend the rest of my life in prison...that's if I'm lucky." His eyes closed briefly. "So you really think that whoever is following you won't question who I am?" He shook his head disdainfully. "No, the problem is that you didn't think at all, did you?"

"I resent that."

He paused for a long moment as he stared at her. "And I resent you, lady. I resent the hell out of you." The bitterness of the words hung between them in the narrow confines of the car. He expelled a long, ragged sigh. "Look," he finally said, "I wasn't ready for you. I knew things wouldn't stay the same, but I hadn't expected you to bring those changes. Do you understand what I'm saying?"

She nodded slowly. "Yes, I think I do. I never expected the changes that happened so quickly in my life, either. I thought I was set. I had money, friends, a place in society...." She laughed lightly. "Everything a girl could want. And then suddenly—pffft!—everything was gone. I had gotten used to the idea that my father was dead, and then I learned that he is very much alive and an international thief." She searched Erickson's eyes in earnest. "I'm only doing what I have to do, John."

His slow, steady gaze swept across her face, centering on the deep green of her eyes. He touched a strand of her hair, concentrating on its texture as it curled between his fingers. "Yes, I know that, Bettina. And I guess that's what worries me. No...it's more than that. It scares the hell out of me."

Chapter Nine

Stephen Bacheller stood in front of the mirror and tried to fasten his bow tie properly. He flubbed up and began again. "You old fool," he grumbled. "Never could do these damned things right." Years ago—too many to count, almost—his wife, Elizabeth, had done this for him. And then when Bettina got older, she had taken over so many of those helpful little practices that women were so good at.

The tie hung loose as his hands dropped to his sides, and his eyes closed. So many memories in that other life, so many remembrances that crowded into his mind, and always at the wrong moment. Tonight was not the time to think about Elizabeth, nor would he think about Bettina and what she must be doing with her life. No, there was too much to do, too much at stake to let sentimentality creep aboard. "Out with you," he cursed, waving his hand distractedly in the air, as if that might help rid his mind of all but practical thoughts of the present.

He adjusted his standing collar and waistcoat, then went back to work on his tie. This time he was reasonably successful. Opening the box in front of him,

A Siren's Lure

he pulled out a dark mustache with flecks of gray in it and squeezed the tube of glue onto the backing. He held the mustache over his upper lip and pressed it into position. Next he opened a jar of cream and, dipping his fingers into it, rubbed the substance through his white hair to darken it and give it a salt-and-pepper shade.

The bathroom door opened and a dark-haired woman appeared, wearing a long, deep-necked sequined gown. She stopped and gaped at his reflection in the mirror. "I—I almost didn't recognize you, Stephen," she said in Italian. "You look so different."

He turned and smiled. "That, *mia cara*, is the idea. Now come here and give me a kiss. Do I not look handsome?"

She hurried over and looped her arms around his neck. "Oh, yes, so very handsome." She stood on tiptoes and pressed her lips to his.

"And you, my sweet maiden, are a vision of loveliness." He reached for the white-and-gold cane leaning against the wall, and took her arm. "Then, shall we go?"

THE NIGHT WAS DARK, the moon and stars veiled by a thin cloud cover. A brisk breeze blew in from the ocean and over the jagged cliffs that had been hollowed by centuries of such winds. There was a salty taste in the air as Bettina and Erickson wound their way through the hilly streets. A cable car had brought them down to the main road from their hotel, which was an old converted convent perched high on a cliff above town.

A Siren's Lure 119

Bettina glanced sideways at Erickson as they walked toward the Lido di Mare. He appeared at ease in his tuxedo. It was hard to imagine that he had spent many of his adult years in drab camouflage outfits or heavy scuba gear, crawling through mud and slime, swimming up onto beaches in the middle of the night to clear away obstacles for ship landings. Tonight, Upton John Erickson looked like a man to whom the easier side of life was as fitting as a well-made leather glove.

They climbed the stairs of the old stone building, its pale pink stucco walls chipped and faded from years of neglect. "Are you sure this is the right place?" Bettina asked, frowning.

He caught her expression and chuckled. "I'm sure."

The ancient carved door swung open, and they were admitted by a woman in a long, silky black dress. Behind her, a burly man stood with his arms crossed, just in case he was called upon to bounce an unwanted guest out on his ear.

Once inside, Bettina realized the interior was nothing like the exterior. Silk walls in a rich forest green and hand-blown crystal chandeliers provided an opulent backdrop for the enormous fortunes won and lost at baccarat, chemin de fer, blackjack and roulette.

"This is a private club," she whispered against Erickson's shoulder. "How did you get us in here?"

"The owner, Vincenzo Cartochetti, owed me."

"Why did he owe you?"

He smiled at her and took her hand, looping it through his arm. "Stop asking so many questions. I want you to smile and be elegant and try to look as if you belong."

120   *A Siren's Lure*

She tilted her chin up at him, her green eyes flashing with cool, iridescent sparks. "I always belong."

His gaze swept over her oyster knit dress, making a slow inspection. A glow warmed the brown centers of his eyes when he noticed the way the dress clung just where it was supposed to, never revealing too much but, instead, giving only a hint of the woman beneath. Her blond hair was pulled back on one side and flowed down her back in soft waves. Her eyes were bright, her skin was smooth and her mouth was coral and inviting. He didn't have to look around the casino to know that she was undoubtedly the most beautiful and elegant woman there. But then, she had also looked as if she belonged perfectly in his wet, oversized T-shirt, leaning up against the sun-baked rocks of the small cove where they had swum. "Yes," he finally said after leisurely drinking in the sight of her, "I'm sure you do."

Her smile was provocative and, he thought, somewhat impish, for Bettina Bacheller no doubt never tired of compliments from men. Despite the havoc she had stirred up in his life and would probably continue to arouse, Erickson was positive he had never seen a more angelic, beguiling face—a face that, in the flash of a smile, could also be seductive and cunning.

He crooked a finger under her chin to lift it. "Remember," he warned softly, "you're along tonight for the ride. We're just going to wander around here and ask a few questions. Nothing heavy or pushy. Don't get your hopes up too high, and don't start any revealing discussions with anyone."

"In other words, Bettina," she murmured flippantly, "keep your eyes open and your mouth shut."

A Siren's Lure 121

He grinned down at her. "You've got it."

For a good part of an hour, they strolled around the casino, pausing at the crap and blackjack tables to watch the thousands of lire pile up on top of one another. Bettina recognized a few faces, mainly those of American movie stars who, like moths, sought out the limelight wherever it might be. Erickson pointed out some of the more famous European opera and stage stars and even spotted the Italian author who sold him the house on Capri.

"Come here," he said, taking her arm. "You want to meet him?"

"I'd love to. Do you think he'll be offended because I haven't read any of his books?"

Erickson smirked. "I doubt it. In fact, he'd probably be shocked if you had. He's sort of the smut king of Italy, real gritty and explicit." He leaned toward her ear. "He's into raw sex."

She twisted her mouth sideways. "You seem to know a great deal about his literary works."

"Of course." He grinned. "I've read every one of his books—several times."

They walked over to the man, and Erickson introduced Bettina. She did her best to follow the conversation, but they were speaking such rapid Italian, she was left behind. However, she had the distinct impression that they were discussing her. The comments appeared to be favorable, although with a smut king, who could tell?

After a few minutes, Erickson took the photograph of Bacheller from his pocket that Bettina had given him. "Have you seen this man around here before?" he asked the writer.

122 *A Siren's Lure*

"No, I am afraid not. He is a friend of yours?"

"My father," Bettina said, entering the conversation, now that she understood the topic.

"Ah. I am sorry, signorina. For you, I wish I had seen this man. But alas, no."

It was the same story all night. They mingled and chatted politely with a number of people, but apparently no one John questioned had seen Stephen Bacheller.

They stood for a while at one of the blackjack tables. Bettina noticed the beautiful young dealer glance up and smile. "Hello, John," she breathed in husky Italian. "It has been a long time."

"Yes," he admitted, smiling back. "It has." He pulled the photo from his pocket and showed it to her. But she, like all the others, only shook her head.

Across the room, an employee of the casino had been keeping a very close eye and ear on the movements and questions of the blond woman and the tall, dark-haired man. Now he walked over to a man with salt-and-pepper hair who was playing chemin de fer with a beautiful woman at his side. The young employee bent down and whispered something in the man's ear, then returned to his post in front of the manager's office.

While Erickson watched the blackjack game, Bettina scanned the room leisurely. Her eyes came to rest on the back of an elegantly dressed man carrying a gold-tipped cane and with a younger woman on his arm. He was walking through the crowd toward the door. Had he been older, Bettina might have thought...No, John was right. She mustn't get her hopes up too high. The man bowed slightly to the re-

A Siren's Lure 123

ceptionist at the door, and the couple went out into the dark night.

Bettina turned back to the table and caught once again the openly inviting looks that the attractive blackjack dealer was sending to John. He winked at the girl and took Bettina's arm, leading her across the room.

"You've been here before," she teased, curious as to the twinges of jealousy she felt.

He gave her a sheepish grin and shrugged. "A few times. I, too, have my weaknesses."

Bettina glanced back at the blackjack dealer, then up at Erickson. "Yes, and I see very clearly what they are."

He stopped and rested his arm on top of an unoccupied slot machine. "You don't approve," he drawled lazily. "And yet I would venture to guess that Bettina Bacheller has her own weaknesses where the male species is concerned."

"Oh? I don't think so."

He smiled. "Of course you wouldn't. But I wouldn't even dare to guess how many men you have charmed with that seductive smile of yours, or how many hearts you have broken with your oh-so-casual indifference."

"Whatever figure you have in your head, I'm quite sure it is an exaggeration."

He pursed his lips as he studied her. "I doubt it."

Her eyes locked with his for a long moment as they both formed a new composite of each other. To Bettina, Upton John Erickson, alias John Stewart, was a dangerously attractive man. She knew he was not the type she should fall for...and she wouldn't. But still, there was something about him that was so compelling, and he appeared to be deliberately reeling her in, even though she was supposed to be the one with the line and hook.

To Erickson, Bettina Bacheller was the most beautiful woman he had ever known. But above and beyond that, she was a dangerous challenge. And if there were two things in his life that he had never been able to avoid, they were danger and a challenge. The fact that she was also beautiful was a temptation too strong for any man to resist.

By the time they had left the casino, the clouds were heavier, and there was a sharp sting in the air. Just as they rounded the corner from the casino, a dark, squatty man stepped in front of them, blocking their path. Bettina felt a cold chill race through her body the minute she heard his low, raspy voice, and she wanted to do nothing more than run.

"Wait, signore, signorina. A moment. I have information that you are looking for."

His voice was like the hiss of a snake, low and grainy and ominous. He spoke so quickly that Bettina could not understand his Italian very well.

Erickson shoved him aside, as if he had no more significance than a pesky fly, and kept walking. But the man and his serpent's voice trailed behind.

"You are looking for a man, no?" When there was no response from Erickson or Bettina, he tried again. "I know of him."

Erickson finally stopped and turned around, glaring down at him. "What kind of information?" he growled.

A Siren's Lure 125

The man's weasellike eyes jumped from Erickson to Bettina, and he repeatedly licked his thick lips. "He was there—tonight."

"Where?"

"In the casino. In the place you just left."

"How do you know who we are looking for?"

"Le Chat Noir, no?"

Bettina's eyes were crinkled in frustration as she looked at Erickson. "What is he saying?"

"He says your father was in the casino tonight."

"What? No! I would have seen him!"

"What did he look like?" Erickson asked.

"He had a woman with him and—"

"I don't want to know about any woman," Erickson cut in sharply. "I want to know about him. What did he look like?"

"He was older, his hair partially gray, his face weathered, but not too much so. He wore a suit—like yours."

"So did ninety percent of the men in there," Erickson grumbled and started to push the man away.

"He had a cane," the man said quickly. "A white cane with a gold tip."

"What did he say?" Bettina asked again. "Did he say something about gold? I don't understand."

Erickson sighed and glanced her way, not putting much stock in what the guy was saying. He never trusted any information that came too easily. But he repeated the man's words to Bettina.

She didn't move. The air left her lungs in a rush. She stared at Erickson, and then her gaze jumped to the man before them. "Did he have a woman with him?" she asked in Italian. "A woman with dark hair?"

126 *A Siren's Lure*

"Sì, signorina."

She turned to John and clutched his arm, her eyes wide and frantic. "I saw that man! I saw him leave the casino. But it couldn't have been—Daddy has much grayer hair and—and it couldn't have been him!"

"Did you see his face?" Erickson asked.

She shook her head. "No, but surely I would have known, wouldn't I? Surely."

Her eyes landed on the man, and she noticed that he was now staring at her openly. His dark eyes had a glazed, frenzied quality about them. Bettina shivered as another wave of chill bumps inched over her flesh.

Erickson caught the direction and intent of the man's leer, and his mouth hardened. "What else do you know about Le Chat Noir?" he snapped.

The man looked back at Erickson, his eyes now blankly innocent. He shrugged. "I know nothing." He stole another glance at Bettina. "But I might know someone who knows something."

Erickson reached into his pocket, pulled out several thousand-lire notes and tossed them at the man's feet. "Looks as if you dropped something," he snarled, but the man just stared down at the pile of money, unmoved. Erickson took out several more and dropped them onto the pile. This time the man fell to his knees and began scooping up the lire. He had just reached for the last note when Erickson's foot captured the hand that clutched and clawed the pavement, his heel grinding into the back of the palm. The man peered up, frightened and in pain. Several drops of sweat rolled down his face.

"Now," Erickson said very calmly and quietly, "who knows something?"

A Siren's Lure 127

"Fa-Father Mangoni," the man groaned, trying to ease his hand from beneath Erickson's foot. It was useless. He was unable to move, and the exertion only added more sweat to his brow. "Norberto Mangoni. He is a priest at the cathedral here." He bobbed his head toward the hill. "Up there, at the top of that long, steep flight of steps."

"What does he know?" Erickson growled.

"I do not know!" the man cried, sweating hard now. "I only know that he has much information about this man you are looking for."

"And if he doesn't?"

"I swear to you! He knows much. I swear it!"

Erickson slid his foot back, and the man slowly stood up. But before he was able to shove all of the money into his pocket, Erickson grabbed him by the collar and slammed him up against the ancient stone wall of the casino building. "If he doesn't, you will hear from me."

"Yes," the man croaked, sliding down the wall after Erickson had released him. Once free, he quickly scrambled to his feet and scurried away into the night.

Bettina leaned back against the wall and let out a deep, ragged breath. She was staring at John with wide eyes, but she didn't even realize it. All she knew was that this was the side of him that Jerry had warned her about, the side she had glimpsed that night he had held a gun on her. There was a violence in him that lay just beneath the surface, ready to spew, and she wondered how much pressure it would take before that violence finally erupted and spilled over to bury her.

But when he rested his forearm against the wall beside her head and angled toward her, there was only warmth and concern in his eyes. There was nothing sinister, nothing threatening. In that moment, he was the most fascinating and attractive man she had ever met in her life. And she asked herself how long she would be able to deny her body what it craved from his touch.

"Whom did he say we need to talk to?" she murmured breathlessly, trying to combat all the reckless urges that he invoked in her.

"Norberto Mangoni, a priest up at the cathedral. Are you okay? You're as white as a sheet."

"Why would a priest know anything about my father?" She ignored his question.

"I don't know, but that's what we're going to find out." He studied her face in the light of the street lamp, then shifted his gaze to her hands, which were pressed flat against the wall. "Did he frighten you?"

"A little," she said, not about to admit that it was he—the man going by the name of John Stewart, the man she wanted to hold and touch right now—who frightened her the most.

"You know, sometimes it's hard for me to imagine that someone has been sheltered as much as you probably have." He lifted his head and stared down the road. "I've seen so much...certain things don't touch me anymore. I forget that for someone like you..." He looked back at her and reached out to stroke her hair near her face. "There is no telling what we'll run into on this search for your father. I've learned to anticipate danger and the unexpected around every corner. And—well, I just want you to know that it's okay to be scared, but you don't need to be afraid. Especially of me."

A Siren's Lure 129

Her breath was held suspended, and her pulse thundered in her ears as his fingers wound like satin ribbons through her hair. "Aren't you ever scared?" she asked weakly.

He rested his hands against the wall, framing her face between them, and leaned toward her. "Constantly. You never lose that. No matter where you are or how good you are at what you do." He paused as his eyes trailed a path down the front of her dress and then rose slowly to her face. His mouth lowered to hers, and he formed the words against her parted lips. "Right now, I'm scared to death."

Her hands were still pressed against the wall at her back, but her face tilted upward to return his kiss. He was warm and persuasive and so utterly male. She breathed in the intoxicating scent of him. When his mouth grazed across her cheek, she expelled a ragged breath and whispered against his skin, "I am not going to become involved with you, John."

He raised his head and looked at her, comparing her remark with her breathlessness and flushed skin. "Why?" he asked softly. "You've been involved with other men, haven't you?"

She closed her eyes briefly before finding the strength to answer. "Other men are safer, more predictable." She opened her eyes and explored his face beneath the facade. "I will not become involved with you."

"You already have." He hesitated, wanting to say more, but he reluctantly straightened up and took her arm. "Now, come on. Let me get you back to the hotel. You've had quite an evening."

130   *A Siren's Lure*

The lift carried them up the rough face of the cliff through the thick vegetation that burst from between the calcareous rocks. A light rain had begun, and it covered the hillside in a silver sheen. The sea lay dark and turbulent behind them as they rose ever higher.

They ran the short distance from the cable car to the hotel, hurrying to get out of the rain. They had climbed the front steps and were about to enter when something made Erickson stop.

"Hurry," Bettina laughingly cried. "I'm soaked!" She finally noticed the strange look on his face and frowned. "What's the matter?"

He was staring through the glass door into the hotel lobby. "We've got trouble."

"Trouble? What do you mean?" She followed his gaze through the doorway to the stairs that led up to the hallway of rooms. At the base of the stairs were two men wearing brown suits.

"Go in and go straight up to your room," John directed.

"But where are you—" Before she could finish asking him where he was going, he had dashed down the steps, rounded the corner of the building, and disappeared. "Of all the nerve," she huffed indignantly, giving the door a hard shove. She walked straight to the front desk and picked up her room key, then headed for the stairs.

"Bettina Bacheller?"

She stopped and faced the two men. Trouble, John had said. What kind of trouble did he mean? "Yes?"

One of the men withdrew a leather badge holder from his pocket and flipped it open. Bettina stared at it, then asked uncertainly, "Interpol?"

A Siren's Lure 131

"Yes."

So that was the kind of trouble John had meant!

"We would like to have a few words with you, signorina, if you don't mind," said the man, whose badge identified him as an inspector.

"And if I do mind?"

"Please, signorina, come with us voluntarily."

Since Bettina had arrived in Italy to find Erickson and search for her father, she had learned to hide some of her nervousness. She attempted to do that now and hoped she could achieve a fair amount of success. "Certainly," she replied calmly. She turned and walked toward the front door, trying to ignore the curious stare of the desk clerk.

As she went out and down the steps, flanked by the men from Interpol, her eyes automatically flicked toward the shadows, seeking out Erickson. That son of a—Why had he gone off and left her like that? If he had used this as his moment to escape, she would kill him. Whatever it took, she would follow him to the ends of the earth!

The police station was in an old white stone building in the center of town. It was small, with a couple of offices to one side of the main room. The men led her into one of these side rooms. It was furnished with a table and a chair, and the inspector politely invited her to sit down.

She sat. The other man quietly left the office and closed the door. *Damn Erickson's hide,* she thought. What did this Interpol inspector want with her? What was he going to do? She had heard too many horror tales of Americans wasting their lives away in foreign jails. But certainly, even if Erickson had deserted her,

132   *A Siren's Lure*

Jerry would come looking for her. He knew both of them were in Amalfi. He would come for her soon. Surely!

"Why are you in Amalfi, signorina?"

She stared into the inspector's cool gray eyes. He was thin, and his gray beard was flecked with raindrops that he had not bothered to wipe away. "I'm touring the coast of Italy," she lied easily.

"Touring?"

"Yes."

"I see. Are you touring alone?"

She paused and gathered her thoughts. "No. I'm with a—a man."

"And where did you meet this man?"

"In Capri."

"His name, please?"

"His name," she repeated dully. "Well, it's a— Malcolm. Yes, Malcolm Gucci."

"Malcolm?" The inspector frowned. "That is an odd name for an Italian, is it not?"

Why was she protecting that bastard? He had left her flat to fend for herself, and here she was, lying for him. How big a hole was she going to dig for herself? "I suppose it is," she answered smoothly. "Maybe— maybe it's not his real name."

"Then you do not know him well?"

"No."

"You are just traveling together and staying in a hotel together?"

She swallowed. "Yes."

"You Americans are a very...friendly people."

She tried to smile, but it was a rather sickly attempt. The air in the room was getting stuffy, and she

A Siren's Lure 133

was finding it increasingly harder to breathe. On the other side of the door, she could hear the light mumble of men's voices and the occasional sound of footsteps striding past.

"Are you familiar with the name Le Chat Noir, Signorina Bacheller?"

She tried to inhale, but only hot air invaded her lungs. "Le Chat Noir? I, ah, well, I think I may have heard the name once or twice. Isn't that...some sort of criminal or something?"

"He is a thief, signorina. A very clever thief. He has struck once again, you know. Today. Here in Amalfi."

"Here! He struck—you mean he stole something from someone here?" Her head began to pound, and she had to wipe her sweating palms along the front of her dress.

"Yes. Interesting, is it not? He has taken a very valuable crown, supposedly the property of the Norman king William II. It was in the Colleta collection here. The Colletas are one of the more illustrious families of this region, and they are quite understandably upset by the loss of this historically important artifact."

"I can imagine," Bettina mumbled, growing sicker by the minute. So her father really had been in Amalfi tonight! And he had come, not for the Festival of La Scala but to steal another priceless objet d'art.

The investigator rested his hands on the table and bent down toward her, his gray eyes capturing her green ones. "Did you know that this man, this Le Chat Noir, is believed to be one of your countrymen?"

"Really?"

134 *A Siren's Lure*

"Yes. And what is even more fascinating is his name."

She was unable to tear her eyes away from that fixed gray stare. She swallowed hard. "His name?"

The man nodded. "Bacheller," he whispered. "Stephen Bacheller. That is your father, no?"

She managed to shake her head. "My father is dead."

"Your father is very much alive and you know it. I believe that is why you are here. You have come to join him, perhaps to work with him."

"No! That's not true!" She sighed and finally dropped her gaze to the hard surface of the table. "I am not a criminal. That is not why I am here." She looked back up. "You must believe me."

"I would like to," he said. "But I would also like to know what it is that you are doing here."

Another man she hadn't seen before walked into the room, after knocking. He began speaking in Italian. "Pardon me, Inspector Aprea, but there is someone here who wishes to speak to you right away."

"Tell him to wait."

"He is with the American government, Inspector. He is here about Signorina Bacheller."

The inspector glanced down at her, his eyes narrowed suspiciously. "Send him in."

Bettina sighed. It was Jerry. He had come for her. He had known somehow that this would happen. Yes, somehow he had anticipated it.

The door swung open, and she couldn't stop the gasp that was forced from her throat. The man who entered wasn't Jerry, but John Erickson.

A Siren's Lure 135

He cast her only a cursory glance before striding briskly over to the inspector, glowering down his nose at the shorter man. "I am Robert Faber, special assistant to the Chief of Missions for the American Embassy in Rome."

The investigator's voice was weary. "Your identification please, signore." Erickson removed a small leather folder from his inside jacket pocket and handed it over. The investigator studied it carefully. Erickson still would not look at Bettina, and her bewildered gaze now volleyed back and forth between the two men. The folder was returned to Erickson, who stuck it back in his pocket.

"I am questioning Signorina Bacheller in connection with a burglary that has taken place here today," the inspector said.

"Miss Bacheller is in Italy at the request of the United States government. She is working for us."

"Doing what?"

"That is not for me to say at this time," Erickson answered stiffly.

"Why was I not informed of this—this situation by your embassy?"

"All in good time, Inspector. All in good time."

Inspector Aprea sighed and sat down on the edge of the table. He did not look at Bettina. "Then there is nothing more I can do tonight. You are free to go, Signorina Bacheller."

She immediately got up and moved around the table to stand next to Erickson. As they walked toward the door, the inspector's voice rang out behind them. "I will call your chief tomorrow," he said. "I expect some answers to my questions. And you, signor-

136 *A Siren's Lure*

ina..." Bettina turned and stared at him across the room. "I must warn you to watch yourself. Getting mixed up with Le Chat Noir could be a very dangerous situation indeed."

Her eyes locked with his for a long moment before jumping to Erickson's tight-lipped expression. Without another word, they left the room and walked out of the police station.

Inspector Aprea remained at the table, musing to himself. His assistant walked into the room and asked him something, but he did not hear. He finally looked up and spoke to the other man. "I want you to keep a very close eye on Signorina Bacheller and her companion. Do not let her out of your sight."

JOHN TOOK THE KEY from Bettina's hand and opened the door to her room. She was in a daze and so exhausted that she had no idea what she was doing.

"How did you do that?" she asked tiredly. "How did you get that identifi—"

"Bettina!" his voice cut in sharply.

Her tired eyes widened in surprise as she saw him press a finger over his mouth. She frowned. It was too much of an effort to figure out what he was trying to tell her. Maybe he thought someone might be listening through the walls. But at this point, she didn't even care.

She dropped onto the bed, too drained even to think about taking off her dress. He came over and sat down beside her. "How did you get that embassy identification?" she whispered.

"Don't ask," he whispered back. "You don't want to know."

She fell back against the bedspread and closed her eyes. "What happened to the dull old parties on Martha's Vineyard?" she mumbled.

Erickson laughed. "Try to get some sleep. Tomorrow is going to be a very busy day." He gently eased her shoes off her feet, then lifted her legs up on the bed. After he had loosened the coverlet from the other side, he draped it over her and dropped a warm kiss on her forehead. Bettina was asleep before he had closed the door behind him.

Chapter Ten

Alvin Bilgeworth crammed a hunk of white cheese into his mouth and wiped his sleeve across his thick lips. A loaf of bread protruded from his jacket pocket, waiting to be devoured. He was standing at the foot of the cable car, resting his weight against a stone wall from which he had a perfect view of the pathway. He was waiting for them to come down from the hotel. And when they did, he would be right behind them. Just as he had been ever since they'd left Capri. Last night he had followed them to the Lido di Mare, but that broad who worked the door and her goon assistant wouldn't let him in. So he had waited. And when they'd left the club, he'd been right behind them again.

Alvin looked at his hands, then tore off a fingernail with his teeth. Hell, he had gotten the same information from the weasel they had talked to. Of course, he had gotten it in a different way. But the point was, he had gotten it. And then, an hour later, he had seen that Bacheller broad with the police, walking to the station. It had been one hell of a busy night. To top it off, he had heard that Le Chat Noir had struck again right here in Amalfi. Right here un-

A Siren's Lure 139

der his nose. He was so close to the bastard, so close, and yet Le Chat Noir had slipped through the collar once again. But Alvin would catch up with him and would either get that necklace back or at least have the pleasure of turning the old man in for the reward. Somehow he would do it. And he was convinced that Bacheller's daughter was his best ticket.

One question still nagged at him. Who was that guy she was with? He was the one in the picture, all right. Alvin had done some snooping around Capri and found out that his name was John Stewart. But something about him didn't sit right. Alvin hadn't been able to work up a profile on the guy's background yet, but he would. He always did. If he could just get the broad alone for a while, he could force all the information he wanted out of her. He smacked his lips. That task would be a real satisfying one.

He pulled the long loaf from his pocket and bit off a hunk, scowling as he chewed. Damned stuff was so dry and hard, he could brick up a house with it. God, he couldn't wait to get back to the good old U.S. of A. and have something decent to eat for a change. He hated this place.

WITH HER HANDS RESTING on the wrought-iron railing, Bettina stood on the balcony and surveyed the town below her and the sea beyond. In the Middle Ages, this seaside resort had been a formidable rival of Genoa and Pisa for control of the Mediterranean. But its importance had been reduced now to serving the tourist trade and to providing a breathtaking view of expensive villas and lush tropical gardens. The wild cliffs and mountains towered on three sides of the vil-

140 *A Siren's Lure*

lage, and the sea lay to the west like a brilliant emerald gem under the early-morning sun. Bettina closed her eyes and took a deep breath of the sea air.

"Buon giorno."

She spun around. John was standing in the opening of her French doors, leaning against the casing, his arms crossed, his eyes sweeping lazily over her.

She was surprised to see him there, but she would have been even more surprised had she known that he had been watching her for some time.

And he had been thoroughly enjoying the view. She was wearing a silky peach robe, held closed only by the sash at her waist. Her hair was freshly washed and hung over her shoulders in soft waves. Her face was free of makeup, her feet bare except for the red polish on the tip of each toenail. While he'd watched her, his mind had been free to wander wherever it wanted to go. In his fantasy, he had walked up to her and carefully pulled loose the sash at her waist, running his hands along her bare flesh. And under the fresh morning sky, with the squall of the birds above them, he had made love to her, the slow erotic kind he had fantasized about since he had first laid eyes on her at the Caffè Solare.

"Good morning," she replied a bit breathlessly, as if she could read his mind. "You—you have a key."

His smile was mellow and pensive. "Yes. You were so out of it last night, I thought you might not wake up this morning without some help, so I picked up a spare from the front desk. But I see that you've been up for a while."

Her gaze swept over the wild landscape. "Yes, it was too beautiful outdoors to sleep." When she looked

A Siren's Lure 141

back at him, his eyes were on the breakfast table in a corner of the balcony. He looked so good this morning, all male, his shoulders broad, his arms tan and with the appearance of almost unlimited strength. "Care to join me?" she asked. "We have freshly squeezed orange juice, croissants, hard rolls, butter, cheese, fruit and tea."

"What, no coffee?" He smiled as he asked this.

"Sorry. You can call and order some if you want."

"We really don't have time."

She frowned as she sat down at the table and began to butter a croissant. "What's the rush?"

He stepped out on the balcony and closed the French doors, making it clear that this conversation was for her ears alone. He picked up a hard roll and tossed it lightly from one hand to the other. "We have to meet Father Mangoni in Pompeii by noon."

"Pompeii! Why there?"

Erickson sat down across from her and split open the roll, spreading some butter on one half. "I went up to the cathedral this morning." He smiled when he noticed her eyes narrow with suspicion. "Thought I'd let you sleep in. The father was just getting on a bus with a group of teenagers he's taking to Pompeii for the day, and he didn't have time to talk."

"But you told him what we wanted to see him about?"

"Yes."

"And what did he say?"

Erickson poured himself a glass of juice and drank half of it before he answered her. "Nothing at first. But finally he agreed to talk to us as long as we did it in Pompeii and not in Amalfi, and especially not at the cathedral.''

Bettina picked up a plum and squeezed it gently. ''He's afraid?''

''Perhaps.''

''So what time do you want to leave?''

His eyes instinctively skimmed across her body once more. ''As soon as you can be ready. I want to be out of town before Inspector Aprea talks to the embassy in Rome. Once he does that, we're in even bigger trouble.''

''Wonderful,'' she murmured, reluctantly setting the plum back on the plate as she stood up. ''I'll get dressed. It won't take long.'' She opened the door and started to step through the opening, but she stopped and turned around to face him. ''I never got to thank you—for rescuing me last night.''

They looked at each other for a highly charged moment.

''So anyway, thank you, John.''

He began a slow study of her, from the top of her head all the way down the silky length of her body, his eyes coming at last to rest on her face. ''You're welcome.''

She stepped through the opening and shut the door behind her. Erickson pushed the roll away from him and leaned back in his chair. He locked his hands behind his neck and stared out over the sea, the same sea that had warned him countless numbers of times in the past few days not to succumb to the lure of this very enticing woman. And he had failed to heed the warnings.

A Siren's Lure 143

THE DRIVE TO POMPEII was uneventful, which in itself was a delight to Bettina. Though she loved adventure and required a fair amount of it in her life, she was beginning to weary a bit of the kaleidoscopic cat-and-mouse routine she and John were playing. She needed fun and excitement, yes, but it would be nice to stop and take a breather once in a while.

In concert with yesterday's drive, an aria from *Rigoletto* was playing on the radio while Erickson's eyes continually darted from the *autostrada* ahead to the *autostrada* behind via the rearview mirror.

"A fat American with receding hair and a double chin. You know him?"

Bettina caught John peering into the rearview mirror and turned around to see the man he was talking about this time. All she could see was a red Fiat with a bad exhaust problem. The car was too far back for her to make out who was driving it. "No," she answered, turning to Erickson. "Is he following us?"

"Yes." And John wondered who the hell he was. Was he with the DIA? He didn't look like Interpol or IRS. He didn't really look like the agency, either, but who knew what kind of stunt they might try to pull to get him back in? He glanced over at Bettina, and his eyes creased in speculation. Who knew what kind of stunt...?

"Do you ever get tired of running?" she asked.

He was surprised by the question and seemed very reluctant to answer it. So she tried again. "Will you tell me why you are running?"

He let out an impatient sigh. "I don't know what you want from me, Bettina. I'm helping you to find your father. What more do you want?"

144 *A Siren's Lure*

"I would like to know you."

"Why?"

"I'm interested."

"I see. Just idle curiosity, is that it?"

"Something like that," she lied easily, knowing inside that it was much more. There were so many elements about him that intrigued her. The hints of danger, the excitement, the adventure, the way he looked. He was so terribly handsome and strong, and she couldn't stop thinking about what it would feel like to have his arms around her and his hands caressing her body. She knew he had a depth of emotion that he kept buried. She could feel it emanating from him, could sense it wanting to escape. It was in his eyes, beneath the brown, buried somewhere deep within the blue. She wanted to see him as he really was. She wanted to know who he really was.

And yet she had meant what she said to him last night. She didn't want to get involved with him. Bettina Bacheller had never been involved with anyone. Her relationships had all been on her terms, short and sweet or short and volatile, but always short. She didn't do well with long-term relationships. She had learned early in life that people she cared about went away. That would never happen again to Bettina, because she would leave them first. But there was something about this man...

She was afraid she would not find it so easy just to walk away from him.

"I was under the impression that you knew everything there was to know about me," he said, his voice acerbic and dry.

"Only speculation and hearsay."

A Siren's Lure 145

The line of his mouth was tight and grim. "Not very pleasant hearsay, I would imagine."

How could she tell him what she knew? Only this morning, while John had been sitting out on her balcony, she had quietly placed a call to Jerry. And Jerry had warned her again not to tell Erickson anything about what the agency knew. He had specifically commanded her not to mention his name. So she would have to keep everything to herself, even though she was rapidly beginning to be weary of that secret, too.

"What's the hardest part of running?" she asked, hoping that by digging into his life, she would be able to divert him from digging too far into hers.

He was very quiet for a long time before answering. "Being a man without a country."

She studied the hard angle of his jaw, the unrelenting profile of an uncompromising man. "You have a country, John. All you have to do is go home."

The hard line broke, but his smile was contemptuous. "You are very naive, Bettina Bacheller. Like most women in the U.S.," he added.

"I see. You've lumped us all together." He didn't answer, but his silence was telling enough. "You sound as if you don't like us very much."

He took his eyes off the road for a moment and glanced at her. She was right. He didn't. And yet this woman sitting next to him, this woman with the blond hair and vivid green eyes and cream-colored skin and open sensuality, did things to the hardened old warrior he had become that he would never have dreamed possible. She brought out a tenderness he thought he had lost the day he left his mother's breast. And she dug up emotions that he believed had died somewhere along the road from one war to the next.

He wasn't at all sure he wanted to bring that part of him back to life again.

AWAKENING FROM A SLUMBER that had lasted nearly eighteen centuries, the ancient city of Pompeii was gradually emerging from beneath its sea of volcanic ash. Roman porticoes, sacrificial altars, luxurious baths and lifelike paintings gave testament to the richness of life that had flourished here so many ages before.

"How are we to find Father Mangoni?" Bettina asked.

Erickson was sitting on a low wall with the map spread out on his lap. "We're to meet him at noon right...let's see, right in here. This is the area that was closed off due to earthquake damage, but he said there was a way to get in there. We're to go through the Forum, which we did, and then up this way past the Stabian Baths, and then..." He stood up and swept his eyes over the area and down the street. "Once we get on the Via degli Augustali, we should see two walls overlapping. Apparently there's a narrow passage through which we can get into the area that's off limits."

"Is all this secrecy really necessary?"

"Look, Bettina, when you want information from someone, you go where they tell you to go. You don't ask too many questions."

They followed the uneven stone streets, passing the remains of bakeries and houses and fountains. The Stabian Baths were on their right.

A Siren's Lure   147

"This is really quite eerie, isn't it? All this opulence and grandeur vanishing the way it did."

"Must have been scarier than hell," he said, concentrating more on the map than on the ruins.

Bettina glanced back up at the now quiet Mount Vesuvius, hovering sleepily behind Pompeii. She thought of the thousands of people whose lives had been snuffed out during the three days that ashes had rained down on the entire Bay of Naples. "Must have been," she murmured.

Erickson stopped walking and pointed across the road. "There it is." With Bettina following him, they walked around the end of one wall and found themselves in the narrow passage that separated the two walls overlapping each other. At the far end of the passage was a slim opening that led into more ruins as far as the eye could see, tumbling, weed-ridden ruins that were under restoration and were therefore off limits to the rest of the touring public.

Erickson checked the map once again. "There's supposedly a house up this road a bit with a large painting of dogs on the walls. He'll meet us there."

It took a quarter of an hour to find the house, but at least they reached it by noon. Bettina sat down on a stone bench. "Do you think he will show?"

Erickson stood with one foot propped up on a fallen pillar and shrugged. "I hope so."

She looked up at him. The sun rode high on his back and cast his long shadow across the grassy ruins. Suddenly she had a vision of him as a Roman gladiator, a warrior of incomparable strength and agility, pleasing a crowded amphitheater with his virility.

148 *A Siren's Lure*

She chuckled lightly. "You know, last night when I was at the police station, I kind of figured you would use that opportunity to get away from me." She smiled again. "I figured you had taken off for—for Madagascar."

He laughed. "Madagascar again, is it?"

She shrugged. "It's the most faraway place I know of."

He was watching her with that same wide, lazy smile on his face that always caused her body to quicken. "It's known as the land at the end of the earth," he said. "A sort of Shangri-la and Lost World, did you know that?"

She shook her head, then closed her eyes and tilted her head back. "No, but it sounds lovely."

He leaned down, resting his forearm on his propped-up leg, his voice low and warm. "Did you really think I wanted to get away from you that badly?"

She opened her eyes and stared up at him. "I thought you might."

"And do you still?"

She tried to even out her breathing, but he was so close, so big, so handsome, and she knew he could probably hear the agitated pounding of her heart. The sound of footfalls tapping against the worn stone road brought her out of the trance she was in, and she turned her head to see a man in a black sweater and slacks approaching them.

Father Norberto Mangoni was a round little man somewhere in his sixties. He had a nose that looked as if it had been broken at one time or another. His large eyes appeared to be staring right through Bettina to the

A Siren's Lure 149

bottom of her soul in examination of her conscience, which had grown almost unbearable to live with.

"I have only a few moments," he explained in Italian. "My young people are anxious to see some of the famous pornographic paintings of Pompeii, and I do not trust them to be on their own for too long." His gaze grew intent upon Bettina's face. "I understand you have a personal interest in finding Le Chat Noir."

"Yes, Father," she answered. He had spoken slowly and distinctly, and she'd been able to understand the gist of what he was saying, but she decided to let Erickson do most of the talking.

"We understand you might have knowledge of him," Erickson said. "Of where he might go next. Is this true?"

Father Mangoni's expression was thoughtful as he looked from one to the other. He might have been in a hurry to get back to his students, but he was not in any hurry to speak. "I believe so," he said finally. "Let us walk."

They started off through the grass-covered ruins, winding in and out of the labyrinth of streets and walkways.

"Do you know the history of my country?" he asked Bettina.

"Only a little," she answered truthfully. History, as well as geography, had never been her strong suit.

"After the fall of the Roman Empire, there was a series of political struggles—first threats from Constantinople and then the barbarian invasions from the north. It wasn't until 1870 that Italy had any real political unity again." He looked from Bettina to Erickson and back to Bettina again. "You need to know this to understand how seriously we take our history and what it has left us.

"During the eleventh century, another foreign power became very prominent in southern Italy. These foreigners were the Normans. They were mercenaries of the Greeks and the Lombards and gradually began to demand territory in payment for their war exploits. In 1130, their leader, Roger II, son of the Norman conqueror Roger Guiscard, was crowned king of Sicily.

"But even so, Constantinople still retained its seat as the cradle of Byzantine art and architecture, and exported its style throughout much of the West. In Palermo, the Norman rulers blended it with their Moorish background, giving the art a very exotic flavor."

He paused to rest and sat down on a low bench that had been in that same spot for almost two thousand years. "One of the most impressive of these Norman blends is in Monreale, Sicily," he said. "From Cefalù to Palermo, all along the northern coast of Sicily, are mosaics of the highest quality. William II, who was king of Sicily during a later period, began the construction of the Cathedral of Monreale in 1174. It is famous for its vast expanses of mosaic, its bronze doors and its delicate cloister. He also built a palace there. Because he was always under pressure from attack by the Arab Moslems, he decided—or at least it is rumored that it was he—but anyway, someone decided to bury many of the royal valuables and works of art beneath the palace and the cloister.

"During successive invasions of the island, as well as fires and...and other acts of God, the cathedral and

A Siren's Lure 151

some of the surrounding buildings were looted. Many of the priceless icons and art objects were stolen. Only three of those have been located to this day. One belonged to a family in Firenze named Ruocco. It was a mosaic of the Annunciation." Father Mangoni looked at Bettina and then at Erickson. "It was stolen last month."

Bettina's face grew pale. "By Le Chat Noir?"

He nodded slowly. "It is believed so. And then only yesterday, the Colletas in Amalfi lost a jewel-encrusted crown that supposedly once belonged to William II. That, too, was one of the items stolen from Monreale."

"You said there were three items that had been located," Erickson interjected.

"Yes, there is one other."

"And where is it?"

"The other piece is a set of carved, gold-plated angels that are in the private collection of a family named Parigi in Cefalù."

Bettina turned to Erickson. "Where is Cefalù?" Her understanding of the priest's explanation of Italian history had not included geographical details.

"Sicily," he replied offhandedly, for he was staring hard at the priest. "How is it that you have all this information? Le Chat Noir stole the crown only yesterday, and yet last night we were given your name. What is your interest in this?"

Father Mangoni smiled at John. "Before I took my position as a priest in the Cathedral of Amalfi, I was a medieval scholar—a historian, if you will. I did much study at the Cathedral in Monreale and I have always been troubled by the loss of artworks that be-

152   *A Siren's Lure*

longed there, that should have remained there. Last month, after the Annunciation was stolen from Firenze, I happened to meet with a priest of the Cathedral of Monreale when we were both in Rome. We were discussing why that particular piece was taken from the Ruocco collection and nothing else. It struck us as odd. And then we began to think that perhaps the crown would soon be stolen from Amalfi. If so, the pattern would indicate that this thief would go to Cefalù next.''

"And the man who met us outside the casino last night? Who was he?"

Father Mangoni waved his hand distractedly. "Oh, he is a young man who cleans up at the cathedral. He does odd jobs for me and—well, who knows what else he does in his spare time. I had heard that the international police were in Amalfi and were looking for this Chat Noir. Emilio—the man you met last night— overheard me talking to someone about it, saying that I had a suspicion the thief would go after the crown next." Norberto Mangoni shrugged. "So Emilio wanted to make some spare change. For that, I cannot condemn him. And it is true, I would like to see this man caught." His gaze jumped to Bettina. "I am sorry to have to say that to you, but I shudder to think what he might do with these historic items he has taken."

"So you don't have any guess as to what he'll do with them now?" Erickson asked.

"No, that I do not know. Many collectors would pay much money to have them in their own collections. Perhaps he is selling them to one of those people. But this I do know..." He paused, his glance

A Siren's Lure 153

jumping once more to Bettina. "I must tell you this. If Le Chat Noir succeeds in getting the angels from the Parigis in Cefalù, he will find himself in very deep trouble. Much worse than he is in already."

"Why?" Bettina asked.

Erickson was frowning. "I've heard that name."

"Yes." Father Mangoni nodded. "I am sure you have. The Parigis are a family with very strong ties to the brotherhood in Palermo. To have Interpol after this thief is one thing, but the Cosa Nostra is an entirely different matter. And now, that is all I know. I really must go back to my students before they tear down the walls of the city to see the erotic works of art."

Bettina held out her hand to him. "Thank you, Father. From all that you've told me, I, too, would like to see the icons returned to Monreale."

"You're welcome, signorina." He turned and nodded to Erickson. "Good luck to you."

The sun was hanging midway in the western sky, angling across the battered ruins, illuminating the Pompeian red of the walls and pillars. Bettina sat down on a fallen column and stared at the dust under her feet.

Erickson was watching her silently, taking note of the discouragement in the sag of her features. "Well," he finally said in a soft, gentle tone, "where shall we go? Madagascar or Sicily?"

"Maybe he really doesn't want me to find him," she said to the dirt in front of her. "It's been seven years. Maybe he honestly doesn't want to see me."

"Maybe not," Erickson replied.

154   *A Siren's Lure*

She sat there, silent and brooding, for several minutes. "But his estate," she said after a while. "I—I have to talk to him and find out what to do." She looked up at Erickson. "This is going to sound stupid to you, but I don't know how to be poor. I—I really don't."

"It doesn't sound stupid. But there are worse things in life than being poor."

"Name one."

He thought for a minute and then laughed.

"See?" She smiled weakly. "You can't think of anything, either. Oh, damn, what am I to do? He might get into terrible trouble down there in Sicily. The priest was talking about the Mafia! I have to find him, John."

"Listen, Bettina, if your father finds himself embroiled with the Mafia, there isn't a whole hell of a lot you can do about it." He squatted down on his heels in front of her and laid his hands on the tops of her thighs. "Look, something is bound to happen to him sooner or later. He cannot keep this up. You do realize that, don't you?"

She was staring directly into his eyes, but she didn't answer.

"Bettina, a man cannot live that way for very long. I speak from experience. Eventually, his own human foibles are going to catch up with him." Erickson took a deep breath and tried to harden himself against the mournful look in the green depths of her eyes. "Maybe you should go home, honey. Try to pick up the pieces on your own. It's only going to hurt more when something does finally happen to him."

A Siren's Lure   155

She swallowed to hold back the tears. "I understand what you're saying, John. But how can I turn my back on him now?" She shook her head. "I can't. However, you've helped me figure out where he is, and for that I'm grateful, but I don't expect you to help anymore. I can take it from here, and you can go back to Capri."

He stared at her, his expression thoughtful. He was free. Free from whatever other traps she might drag him into. He could go back to Capri and pick up where he had left off. Maybe no one had gotten wind of who he was. And she was right; he had done more than his share. He should take advantage of her suggestion and get away.

He studied her face. It was pale and sad, but at the same time, it was set with a determination that he couldn't help but admire. He let out a slow, tired breath. He could not leave her. He knew that. He also knew that somewhere down the line—sometime soon—he was going to regret this decision. But he couldn't leave her. Not yet.

"And what happens if Interpol picks you up again?" he asked, with a gentle smile playing around his mouth. "Who's going to bail you out of trouble?"

Instinctively, her chin lifted in a proud angle. "I can manage."

"Sure you can. But what are you going to do when they stick bamboo splints under your nails and ask you about me?"

She couldn't stop the smile that came to her lips.

"You might spill the beans about me," he said.

156   *A Siren's Lure*

She pursed her lips and gazed up at him, his broad shoulders framed by the afternoon light. "I just might."

He shrugged. "See, I can't take that chance. I'm not letting you out of my sight until I have you on a plane back to the States."

Her newly found conscience rumbled within her. She had tricked him and no doubt she would continue to deceive him. After all, she owed Jerry something for pointing her in Erickson's direction in the first place. If it hadn't been for Jerry, she wouldn't have gotten this far. But as she gazed up into Erickson's strong, handsome face and into those eyes that were filled with so many compelling secrets, she wondered how long she could keep up the masquerade. "Are you sure about this?"

"I'm sure," he lied, then reached for her hand. "So," he said with a sigh. "I guess this means Shangri-la will have to wait."

She sighed, too. "Bye-bye, Shangri-la."

Turning away from her, he noticed two men standing by the ruins of an ancient bakery a hundred yards away. There was a certain look about undercover police or government agents that was a dead giveaway. The minute he spotted them, Erickson knew they weren't tourists—and the fact that one of them had a camera raised and pointed directly at him reinforced his suspicion. There were only two of them there, but he wondered how many more were behind him, or waiting in the parking lot, or ready to follow him and Bettina down the *autostrade*. He also wondered whether these men were after him or after Bettina.

Either way, he would be the biggest loser, locked up in the prison he had been running from for five years.

He glanced down at her, innocently oblivious to the net that was closing in around them. "Hello, Sicily," he mumbled dryly, aware that there was a very good chance they wouldn't even make it halfway there.

Chapter Eleven

The sun was low in the sky. The warmth of it penetrated through Bettina's side of the car, through the glass, filling her body with a delicious sensation. The soothing strains of Vivaldi from the stereo speakers lulled her into a hypnotic state. She felt relaxed and at peace. Her eyes were closed and a soft smile played on her lips.

Suddenly she was thrown sideways, and her head knocked against the window. Instinctively she grabbed for the padded door handle with one hand and the edge of the seat with the other. Her eyes flew open. The sound of the car shifting into a lower gear vibrated upward through her body.

She was thrown again, but his time she was able to hold herself steadier. She glanced at Erickson and saw the grim set of his jaw, the determined profile chiseled from granite. He swerved to the right this time, and she was thrown toward him.

"What—what are you doing!" Her voice sounded foolishly sleepy to her own ears. A car horn blared beside her, and she jumped as John skimmed past the vehicle, almost sideswiping its frame. "Wh-what...?"

A Siren's Lure 159

"Bettina, I want you to wake up and listen to me carefully." He sent a cursory glance her way. "Are you awake?"

"How could I be otherwise?" She grimaced, holding tight to the seat as he squealed around another corner. "This is crazy! We're going to be—" a truck was barreling down on them from a side street; Bettina screamed as it veered to the left only seconds before it would have smashed into her door "—killed!"

They were in downtown Salerno…she thought. But maybe she had been asleep longer than she realized. She didn't really know where they were. All she knew was that Erickson was driving like a bat that had just been released from the gates of hell and that they were probably going to end up in a flaming pile of metal if he didn't slow down.

He laid on the horn as he careened through a traffic light, dodging in and out of the heavy flow of cars. "Now, do exactly as I say." He didn't look at her. All of his attention was focused on the road ahead, with an occasional glance in the rearview mirror.

Her heart was drumming loudly now, and the sounds of Vivaldi were drowned out by the blaring of horns and the squeal of tires. "I'm going to stop the car at the train station. I want you to run inside to the ticket counter and get us on the Peloritano. The *rapido* to Messina. Book a sleeper."

"A train?" Her breath was suddenly sucked in as he swerved around a bus, missing the front end of it by a hair's width. The air came out of her lungs in a loud whoosh. They had a car. What did they need a train for?

160 *A Siren's Lure*

"The Peloritano," he repeated harshly, grating her already exposed nerves. He saw the look on her face and drew his mouth into a sharp, thin line. "If you want to find your old man, don't ask questions. Just do it."

"Okay," she managed, trying to turn around in her seat to see if someone was following them. The swiveling action made her stomach churn. She had never been good with a lot of motion. And this was enough motion to make her lose the entire contents of her stomach.

"I'll get the bags," he was saying. "And I'll try to divert the tail." He slapped his hand on the horn as a car pulled in front of them, forcing him to slow down. "Ah, dammit, get out my way!" He veered right and pressed his foot to the pedal, hauling past the other car and swerving in front of it. The tires squealed loudly as he skidded around the next corner, and she heard the case of wine in the backseat hit the floor. "As soon as you have the tickets, get on the train. I'll meet you there."

She took the chance of loosening her grip on the seat edge so that she could find her shoes on the floorboard and slip them on. But when he slammed on the brakes for a pedestrian, she was thrown against the dash. She caught herself at the last second, and her forehead hit the backs of her hands instead of the hard vinyl.

"Don't stop for anyone or anything, Bettina. You got that?"

She put her shoes on quickly and gathered up her purse and sweater. "Is someone following us?" she yelled over the blare of his horn.

A Siren's Lure 161

He ignored her as he jammed the gas pedal down and skidded into the parking lot of the station. "Okay," he commanded. "Go!"

She jumped out, amazed at her speed in doing so, and automatically searched left and right. The station was in front of her, so she ran. Cars were everywhere and she had to dodge them. Her heel slipped out of one shoe and her purse banged against her side as she ran, hobbling and gasping, clutching the sweater tightly in her clenched fist.

She couldn't think about why she was running. There wasn't time. All she knew was that John had said to do it, and his commands were nothing to argue with. He had said to do it. She was doing it.

She dashed up the stairs of the building and shoved through the doors, almost knocking down an elderly woman who was pushing a big cart of luggage out the door. Bettina didn't stop to help. There was no time.

Her eyes darted back and forth, frantic in their search for a ticket counter. He had told her to hurry. He had told her to go right to the ticket counter. But where the hell was it?

She finally spotted one about fifty feet away. She ran toward it, weaving in and out of the crowd, unmindful of the attention she was drawing. The din of announcements and screaming trains was almost deafening. She reached the counter, but there was a long line of people waiting. Her heart was pounding. Her lungs hurt. She didn't know what she was doing or why she was doing it. Who were they running from and why did there have to be such a long line at this counter? Why didn't these people stay home and get out of her way!

162   *A Siren's Lure*

She shifted back and forth on her feet, indecision in her every breath. Her eyes scanned the large room and she saw another ticket counter. She left the line she was in and hurried over to it, bumping into a man so hard that she knocked the briefcase out of his hand.

"Oh—I'm sorry—*mi scusi, mi—*" She turned back around and continued toward the other counter. She finally reached it. It, too, had a long line, but not as long as the other one. She shifted nervously from one foot to the other, her head swiveling back and forth as she sought out this unknown person or thing she was supposedly running from.

She was hot. A band of sweat lay heavy against the back of her neck. She was scared. At this point, she couldn't distinguish between fear for herself or fear for Erickson. All she knew was that she was so scared she could feel the blood pounding in her temples and could hear her knees shaking.

She couldn't take the waiting any longer; she would never get their tickets at this rate. Shoving her way through the throng of people and luggage, she edged up to the front of the line, cringing at the loud, expressive curses that were directed at her back.

"*Per favore...per favore, due...*ah...*due* tickets—" Oh, hell, she couldn't even remember any Italian. "*Biglietto! Due bigliettos.*" Oh, but what train had John said? The Positani? No. The Peritoni? Her eyes scanned the wall behind the counter, reading the schedule as quickly as she could. There it was. The Peloritano. "*Il Peloritano. Due per un...un—*" What was that blasted word for first-class sleeper? "*Un...prima classe...*ah, sleeper, you know, to sleep? Ah, *vagone, vagone letto!*" she cried, exulted by her

A Siren's Lure 163

ability to remember. So proud was she that she didn't even hear the ripple of laughter in the line behind her.

The ticket agent stared back at her, bored by her recitation. "Where are you going?"

Her mouth fell open. Why hadn't he told her he spoke English? "Messina," she ground out through clenched teeth, her mouth tight, her cheeks flushed. "And hurry."

"Four hundred and thirty thousand, two hundred and forty-eight lire," he mumbled, writing up the tickets for her.

She shifted her sweater to the other arm, opened her purse and riffled through it until she came up with a large wad of bills. She handed it to him, and he took great pains to count it out slowly and carefully. "Could you hurry, please!" she snapped, but he gave her a long, bored look and continued counting the money in his deliberate way.

Finally he handed the tickets to her.

"Which platform?"

His eyes grew blank.

"Su quale binario!" she yelled, slapping her flattened palm on the counter.

"Ah." He nodded slowly. *"Numero otto."* He smiled mischievously. "But you had better hurry. It leaves in less than five minutes."

She glared at him for a hostile moment, then pivoted on her heels and pushed back through the pressing line. The smells and the heat from the crowd were oppressive. A train whistle blew in the distance. Somewhere a speaker was blaring music, but it sounded scratchy and disconnected. Platform number eight. Her eyes moved frantically to the signs

164 *A Siren's Lure*

overhead. Number six, seven…there it was. At the far end.

She stopped again to adjust her loose shoe, just as a hand reached out for her. She flinched and drew back, staring into a pair of cold, washed-out eyes. The man grinned crookedly at her, and the sight of it chilled her to the bone. She spun around and ran away from him as fast as she could. That fat man—she knew him from somewhere. Well, not knew him, really. She had seen him. But where?

She passed platform seven. The sound of the speaker overhead was loud in her ear. She couldn't understand anything that was being said. The words echoed along the cavernous walls, reverberating in her brain. She was almost to platform eight. Fat man…an ice cream cone…Amalfi…Capri…in front of her hotel in Washington…a fat man with receding hair. Erickson had said it. He had asked her if she knew such a person, fat man with receding hair. She did know him! She had seen him! Everywhere!

She glanced back over her shoulder but didn't see him behind her. Yes, now there he was. She tripped and two hands reached out to catch her fall. A man. She stumbled to her feet and continued running, through the large doorway that led to number eight. The smells of metal and dirt and sweat wrapped like a heavy cloud around her. She could taste the diesel fuel in the back of her mouth. Her lungs felt like exploding. Her legs were tired.

She glanced behind her but didn't see him. She had lost him. He had lost her. She reached out for the railing and jumped onto the train, clutching the conductor's arm. He was frowning at her, but she was too

A Siren's Lure

breathless to speak. She handed him the ticket, and he answered in rapid Italian. She understood enough to know that she was in the wrong car. "Which car?" she managed to ask.

He answered, but she didn't like what she heard. Four cars down. She would have to get off the train and walk down the platform. Maybe she'd run into that man again. She stood on the step of the car, undecided. Several people were waiting to get on, so she had to make a decision fast. She would go through from the interior, cross from car to car over the couplings.

She climbed back up into the train and hurried down the length of the car, trying to dodge the other passengers who were making their way to their seats. She pulled open the door and held her breath as a waft of diesel fuel hit her full force in the face. The sounds of the stations were magnified from this spot, and she automatically cringed at the hissing, screaming noise. She moved into the next car and forged her way down its length.

She reached the next door and stopped. He was there. The fat man with the pale eyes. On the platform. Heading this way. He was looking up into the windows of the train as he passed, searching for her, so she hung back against the wall inside the door, her throat constricted, her breath held back in her lungs. She sneaked a look out and didn't see him again, so she carefully opened the door and stepped out onto the coupling. As soon as she was safely inside the next car, she ran the length of it, wending her way through a line of people heading for their own sleeper compartments.

166 *A Siren's Lure*

She didn't see him now, so she hurried into the fourth car. A conductor was there, and she grabbed hold of his shirt sleeve. She assumed that he would easily see the panic in her face and say something, offer help—anything. But he quite calmly directed her to her compartment and then slipped by her to assist the next passenger.

She reached her compartment and turned the knob, moving quickly inside and slamming the door behind her. Her back was against it. Her breath was faint and quick. Her eyes stung from the cloud of smoke on the platform, and her ears still rang with the echo of the noise in the station. She could hear people climbing aboard, clomping down the corridor, closing the doors of their compartments.

She closed her eyes and leaned her head back. Where was John? He said he would get the bags and...what had he said? Lose the tail? But if it was this fat man who was following them, then Erickson hadn't lost him at all. Where was John? Why wasn't he here by now?

She opened her eyes, and the shock of what she saw slammed her up flat against the door, her hands pressed against the metal, her eyes and mouth wide with fear.

The man was standing just outside her window, staring in at her from the platform. He grinned perversely and then moved out of sight.

Bettina stood frozen to the spot. Her fear held her immobile. He had seen her. He knew where she was. What did he want with her?

A Siren's Lure

She heard a loud, clomping sound down the corridor. It came closer, then stopped outside her door. The doorknob twisted behind the small of her back.

She jumped at the contact and spun around, grabbing hold of the doorknob to hold it still. She wasn't going to let him in. She would hold the knob so tight he would never be able to turn it.

As it continued to twist beneath her hands, she lifted her eyes to the bolt above the knob and gasped. How could she have forgotten to do such an elementary thing as locking the door?

If she could just lift her hands away from the knob, she could shoot the bolt home. But she would have to do it fast. Very fast.

Swallowing the fear, she took her hands away from the knob and lifted them to the bolt. She tried to turn it, but her fingers were shaking so badly she couldn't make it move. The knob turned again, and this time it clicked. She felt the pressure of the door opening. She kept her body against it to hold it closed, but the man was too strong for her. With one heavy shove, he had the door open and was standing in front of her, pointing a large revolver at her chest.

She backed across the compartment and bumped into the wall, staring transfixed at the weapon in his hands. She couldn't even think; her brain was too clogged.

The window was behind her back. If she could just open it and...But why couldn't she scream? Her throat was tight. A cold hand of terror reached through her flesh and clutched her bones.

Instinctively, she reached for something to throw, but the only things that weren't bolted down were her

168 *A Siren's Lure*

handbag and sweater. She lifted the purse swiftly and hurled it toward him. Like a flying missile, it struck his stomach but glanced off and fell to the floor.

He laughed and leaned back against the door, fastening the bolt behind his back. At the click of the lock, the cold fingers inside her inched their way up her spine.

"Who—who are you?" she spat through bared teeth. "What do you want?"

His smile was crooked and decidedly ugly. His body and face were fat, and his neck was so short he appeared not to have one at all. Sparse hair stuck straight out from above his too-large ears, and his stomach hung like a balloon over his low-slung belt.

But it was the gun in his mouth that she stared at. Despite the gun he held on her, despite the despicable appearance he presented, what kept her eyes riveted on his face was the fact that he was standing there casually chewing bubble gum.

"Alvin's the name," he said while chewing. "Alvin Bilgeworth."

"If it's money you want..."

He laughed again. "Oh, it's money all right." He blew a huge bubble, and it popped all around his mouth. His tongue snaked out to eat it off his upper lip. "And you, sweet pea, are gonna lead me right to it."

Her sweater had fallen to the floor, and her purse lay at his feet. Her hands repeatedly clenched in front of her, and she felt a trickle of sweat run down the front of her blouse. "What do you mean?" Oh, she sounded so calm now, so collected. There was no tremor to her voice, no fear that she could detect. Only

A Siren's Lure 169

that stream of perspiration dripping steadily down her chest beneath the cotton blouse.

"I mean, sugar britches, you're gonna lead me to your old man. I take it you know where he is by now. That is, you and your boyfriend, who, by the way, didn't seem to make it."

For the first time, Bettina was aware of a slow, gentle rocking as the train edged its way out of the tunnel. Her calm, collected facade began to crumble. John hadn't made it. He had missed the train. He had left her to face this man alone.

"Toooo bad," he crooned, mocking her. "Looks like it's just you and me, baby doll." She cringed as his eyes flicked to the bed and then back to her. "And a nice, long night ahead of us."

The wad of fear was beginning to congeal. It was gumming up into a tight, hard ball in the pit of her stomach. She was aware of the loud clacking of the wheels as the train picked up speed, the hiss of the engines, the rhythmic thud against the tracks.

Bilgeworth laughed again, this time cruelly. "Yep, I've been on you for a long time, honey bunch. A long time."

Her breath came out in a loud exhalation. She had to do something. She couldn't just stand there and let this obscene man have the upper edge. She had to think!

"What do you want with my father?" She had to talk to him, keep him occupied until she could think of something to do, some way to get away from him.

He stepped over to her and pressed the tip of the gun into her stomach. Her breath locked in her throat; her

170   *A Siren's Lure*

skin felt clammy and cold. "You ever heard of Hopkins Mutual?"

Her brain was barely functioning. But she had to force it open. She had to listen. Had to talk. "Yes. It's...a...a large insurance company, isn't it?"

"The biggest, baby." He shrugged. "Next to Lloyd's of London, that is." His breath was hot and released in quick, labored pants. For the first time, she realized that he, too, was afraid. That bit of knowledge alone unblocked the dam in the back of her throat and made it possible for her to breathe more easily. He was just as afraid as she was. She could see the sweat on his temples, the line of moisture above his upper lip. The gun was unsteady in his hand, the tip quivering against her stomach. He was afraid, too!

"Your old man stole something from one of their clients," he said, shoving the gun harder into her stomach. "They hired me to get it back."

Her stomach hurt where the metal shaft pressed into it, but her attention was riveted on his face. Why would a company like Hopkins Mutual—or any company for that matter—hire such a grotesque slob to do anything?

He was only inches away and looked at her with an ugly sneer. "Don't let the veneer fool you, honey," he said, reading her mind. "Alvin Bilgeworth always delivers the good."

They heard the footsteps at the same time—clicking down the corridor; pausing outside the door. Her skin started to tingle, but whether from fear or anticipation, she didn't know.

In one swift movement, Alvin was behind her, his arm wrapped around her chest and shoulders, the gun

A Siren's Lure 171

held taut at the base of her skull. "Keep your mouth shut," he whispered frantically.

She nodded, panic forcing any other alternative from her mind.

"Don't make a move," he said, pushing her head with the gun to reinforce his power over her.

Suddenly something inside her snapped. It came to her in a flash, like the sudden light and crack of lightning before the ominous roll of thunder. The fear moved aside, making way for the anger. In the past two weeks she had been evicted from her home by the IRS, threatened by a commando fighter on the lam and interrogated by two Interpol agents. Now she was being victimized by a viciously cruel insurance investigator. Threatened, frightened, scared out of her wits, pushed around...

The thunder reached a feverish pitch inside her body and mind, catapulting outward to her throat and hand and legs. No one threatened Bettina Bacheller. No one!

The scream burst forth from her throat and caught Bilgeworth by surprise. Her arm came up and her elbow connected with his chin. He stumbled backward, the gun waving frantically. A gunshot splintered the air, and the door crashed open. Another shot exploded. Bettina screamed until she thought the sound would echo in her head forever.

She was pressed back against the wall as Erickson, looming larger than life in the doorway, threw himself across the room and pounced on Alvin Bilgeworth. He picked him up, flung him against the wall, then dragged him out the door. Bettina could hear a strange gurgling noise coming from the fat man's

172 *A Siren's Lure*

throat. She ran to the door, clinging to the casing as she stared after them. Several passengers had opened their doors and were gawking mutely at the two men hurtling down the corridor, one dragging the other along the floor. The door at the end of the car was open, and Erickson shoved Alvin out onto the coupling.

Bettina squeezed her eyes shut when she heard several loud yells. This time when she screamed, she clamped her hand tightly over her mouth to hold the terror in.

Her fingers were pressing hard into her cheek as she watched Erickson stomp back down the corridor. He glared at the inquisitive passengers, shoved his way back into the compartment and slammed the door.

Bettina had jumped out of his way and was standing by the bunk beds, clutching a rung of the ladder for support. "Is he...dead?" she squeaked.

Erickson's breath was coming hard and fast as he leaned against the door and stared at her. "Do you care?"

She nodded weakly. "Yes."

He studied her closely—her pale face, her wet eyes, her tear-streaked cheeks. "He's not dead."

She watched the rapid rise and fall of his chest. She was shaking and her throat ached from screaming. But she couldn't say anything. She couldn't take her eyes off him.

Finally, something broke and she ran to him, falling into his waiting arms, her sobs muffled against the warmth of his shirt. His hand was in her hair, soothing, caressing, as he breathlessly tried to whisper reassurances to her. She could feel the pistol and holster

A Siren's Lure

beneath his shirt; it pressed almost painfully into her chest. But she didn't care. His mouth touched the top of her head, and his hands stroked her hair and back. She wanted their closeness to go on forever.

"Who was he?" he whispered, his face against the top of her head.

She didn't lift her head or try to pull away. Instead, she spoke against his shirt, her voice shaky and weak. "He—he—I guess he's an insurance investigator with—with Hopkins Mutual." Another sob broke from her, and several seconds passed before she regained her voice. "I figured there were some insurance people looking for my father, but—but I had no idea who." At last she lifted her head to peer up at him beseechingly, as if he might not believe her. "I had no idea, John."

He rested her head against his chest and brushed her hair with his fingers. "I believe you," he murmured.

He held her tight, his own fear for her still rolling through him like a thunderous cloud. He'd been sure he had lost the two government agents who were following them, but when he had seen that fat guy getting on the train, John had been halfway across the station and couldn't reach Bilgeworth in time. He had known so many kinds of fear in his life as a soldier and as a man on the run. But for the first time today, he had been afraid for a woman. His own fears for himself had for once been secondary. He had been afraid for Bettina.

She shivered as the images of that grotesque man came back to her with full force. "He said he had been following me for a long time. I remember seeing him before. I remember—one night he was standing out-

side my house. He's been following me everywhere."
She glanced up at Erickson. "It's awful, knowing that
someone is following you, isn't it?"

He nodded his head. "Yes, it is."

She glanced down at the floor. The two bags had
been thrown haphazardly into the compartment when
he had come charging in after Alvin. "I see you got
our luggage."

He was watching her as she looked up at him, neither of them quite sure what to do or say next.

She kept her eyes trained on him, but her voice was
still soft and tentative. "I was so afraid you had
missed the train. He had a gun and he was..." She
sighed heavily and shifted her eyes toward the window. "I'm afraid I'm not very good at all this cloak-
and-dagger stuff."

"You're doing just fine, Bettina. I'm the one who's
not doing so hot. I should have been here with you. I
shouldn't have let you go...."

She moved away and, holding herself steady against
the wall, stared out at the rapidly approaching night.
Only a slim band of red lingered on the horizon; the
sky above it was dark. The train rocked and swayed
down the track, and the flickering lights of a town
sped by in a blur.

They were safe now. Safe and warm. The two of
them together. Erickson had made it to the train on
time. Alvin Bilgeworth was no longer a threat. They
were alone—just the two of them.

She stayed at the window for a long time. The gentle
shunt of the wheels slowly replaced all the fear in her
body with a new sensation, as if a flame deep within
her body had been lit and was starting to grow.

A Siren's Lure 175

Bettina turned around to see Erickson standing in the same spot. She walked over and stood in front of him, reaching out to grasp the upper bed railing for balance. Her eyes lifted to his face, and she had to search for her breath. "I want to thank you for rescuing me again."

He held his expression in perfect control as he stared at her, but his voice was low and husky. "Anytime."

"You are always there when I..." Her voice trailed off as she studied the fertile brown of his eyes. "John, I—I want to see your eyes...without the contacts."

He flinched in surprise, but only for a moment. The look in his eyes was replaced by something else, a deep hunger that she had glimpsed in him before, but one that she had been afraid to tempt.

"You might not like what you see," he said gruffly.

"Let me be the judge of that."

He studied her for a moment, in a thoughtful and hesitant way, then squatted beside his duffel bag and went through it until he had found a small plastic case. "You know a lot about me, don't you?"

"Yes," she answered honestly.

He stood up and stepped over to the sink with the case. With one last glance in her direction, he bent over and popped the contacts from his eyes, setting them carefully into their special holder. Then he turned around slowly and came back to her, his body only inches from hers.

Bettina was unable to draw her eyes away from him. "God," she breathed softly. His were the most gorgeous eyes she had ever seen. They were like a sea she could drown in, a boundless sapphire sea that was capable of both misty tranquillity and reckless passion.

176   *A Siren's Lure*

And in this moment they were silent, intense and almost fiercely possessive, waiting for her to make the next move.

But he was waiting only because he had lost the ability to act. He kept skimming his eyes over her face, exploring and memorizing the lines and curves, drinking in the ivory color of her skin and the intoxicating fragrance of her perfume. His gaze dropped lower. The train rocked back and forth, and her chest rose and fell at almost the same pace. His own breath accelerated. He lifted his eyes back to her face, and he knew now that she could not mistake what was in them. She had to see the hunger—she had to know how badly he wanted her.

"It's trains," she offered, knowing the excuse sounded as feeble to his ears as it did to hers. Her voice was shallow and weak. "There is—is something.... They have this rhythm that—"

A half-muffled groan ripped from his throat as he pulled her into his arms and fastened his mouth over hers. His kiss was hard and hot and demanding. One hand held her neck; the other was at the small of her back. She was imprisoned by his hands, and the warmth of his fingers spread through her like flame.

She opened herself to him, parting her lips to the savage thrust of his tongue, pressing her breasts against him, even though the gun in its holster gouged into her flesh. Her pulse thundered in her ears; her hands rose encouragingly up the strong arms that held her, and looped possessively around his neck.

He kissed her until she had no breath left, but she moaned when he pulled his mouth away. His lips grazed a searing path across her cheek to the lobe of

A Siren's Lure 177

her ear. "I've wanted you since I first saw you. Did you know that?"

"I thought you hated me," she whispered, loving the sound of his voice, the touch of his hands.

He closed his eyes briefly. "I wanted to hate you. God knows, I wanted to."

"I was very afraid of you then."

His eyes dropped down to the pounding pulse in her throat and then lower still to her body where it conformed to his. He lifted his gaze back to her face, probing very deeply. "You're not afraid of me now, are you?"

His eyes were so blue, so intense, so compelling. How could she be afraid of a man who filled her with the most incredible desires she had ever known? She wasn't afraid of his touch. She wanted it; she needed it. Yes, he was extremely strong and powerful and, at times, violent. But he had never done anything to hurt her. He wanted to make love to her. "No, John, I'm not afraid of you now."

"I won't hurt you."

"I know that." She felt his hand move to her breast, his fingers like hot coals on her blouse. "How—how long do we have?" she whispered breathlessly, on fire for this man she knew so little about and lost within a power that was, for the first time, greater than her own.

"Plenty of time." His voice was a low murmur against her hair. "All night, Bettina." His fingers moved to the top button of her blouse. "As long as you want me."

178 *A Siren's Lure*

HER HEAD WAS CURLED against his arm, and her eyes were closed. He brushed the damp hair back from her face and reached over with his free hand for his shirt on the floor. After pulling out a pack of cigarettes from the shirt pocket, he lit one and lay back quietly. Bettina was nestled along his side, his left arm beneath her shoulders. The moon was up now, hanging in a white crescent over the passing landscape. The sway of the train was soothing, the sound of the wheels against the track a hypnotic song.

After a few minutes, he felt her shiver. "Cold?" he asked, draping his big shirt across her body and pulling her more tightly against his side.

"John?" she said softly, pausing before she went on. "Why did you want to be a soldier?"

He took a long draw on the cigarette and exhaled slowly. An ashtray was on the shelf beside the bed, so he reached for it and set it on the floor beside him, flicking the loose ashes into it. "I don't know," he replied finally. "I guess I was raised to think that a man did that sort of thing. You know, went off to fight so that women like you would be safe."

She tilted her head to look up at him, and she smiled in wonderment. "Do you really believe all that?"

He shrugged. "I guess I did at the time. Why? You don't agree?" His grin was lopsided when he glanced over at her. "I must say you don't seem the feminist type, wanting to march off to war and fight in the trenches with all the other GIs."

She laughed lightly, and he loved the sound of it and the feel of it against the side of his chest. "No," she said. "I kind of like the idea of men taking care of me. They always have."

A Siren's Lure 179

He studied the top of her head, wondering just how many men she had been with and how special they might have been in her life.

She noticed his thoughtful look. "I know what you're thinking," she said, half smiling.

"Oh?"

"Yes. You want to know about other men I've been to bed with."

A muscle snapped in his jaw, and he shook his head roughly. "It doesn't matter."

"Yes, it does," she said. "Or it should. It would if I were in your shoes." She eased her leg up over his thigh. "And the answer to your unasked question is that there haven't been that many and none who...well, who really left much of an impression. The first time, of course, was experimental—for him and for me. And after that was comparison and—I don't know, maybe searching for something, for some connection with someone." Searching for what she had found tonight with John.

He was examining her with eyes that missed very little, but he was unable to show or even admit to any emotion that her words might have stirred. He had been a man within himself for too long. He didn't even know how to break out, let alone want to. But something told him that, with her, he might decide it was worth the risk.

"And what about you?" she ventured, trying to sound more casual than she felt. "A girl in every port?"

He smiled. "A few."

"There must have been some special one somewhere along the way."

180 *A Siren's Lure*

He shook his head. "There wasn't time. I've been on the move most of my adult life." He searched her eyes carefully as he spoke. "I probably always will be."

She chose not to pursue that remark for now. She wasn't really sure how she felt about it, nor had she untwisted her feelings about him enough to know what they meant. "Were you ever in a position where you stayed put for a while?"

He took the last draw on the cigarette and stubbed it out in the ashtray. He exhaled slowly. "If I was, it was before I was eighteen. After that, the world went haywire, and I jumped on the frazzled end of it for a ride. I'm still on it."

She was very quiet for several minutes, but the words in her head and in her heart, she knew, had to be spoken sometime. If not now, then later. "It's hard for me to—to understand...well, all the killing and, ah..."

His jaw had hardened like a rock, and his eyes were as dark as the depths of the ocean. "It's still the efficient assassin, is it? The cold-blooded killer?"

"I didn't say that," she answered defensively, wishing now that she hadn't even brought it up.

"But you think it." His tone was full of self-derision. "And you may be right. But just wait until some Mideast country goes berserk again and takes over another American embassy, or tries to cut off our foreign oil supply. You know who the present administration will call on to help? Us. And then we won't be warmongers or killers or...or hired assassins. We'll be heroes. It's only a matter of time, Bettina. Just a matter of time."

A Siren's Lure 181

She was silent, but after a minute, she turned her head into the side of his hard chest and kissed him. "These companies that you consult with...don't they ever wonder who you are, where you came from, how you know so much about all those countries?" Bending her head, she ran the tip of her tongue along his side, her body electrified by the sharp intake of his breath.

His eyes were closed, his breathing growing labored. "They don't care. All they want is to be able to do business in countries with—" her mouth trailed across the hard plane of his stomach "—the...the least amount of hassle."

She teased a fingernail down his other side and onto the front of his hip. Her mouth slipped lower. "But won't they—"

He let out a low groan and rolled on top of her, his weight pressing her down into the narrow confines of the bed. "You ask a hell of a lot of questions," he growled before clamping his mouth over hers and taking her once again on a long, slow journey of passion.

Chapter Twelve

He rolled over and opened his eyes. The light was coming in through the train window and he saw snow-covered mountains in the distance, green upland meadows dotted with poplar and ash. On the other side of the train would be the Mediterranean. His eyes swung to Bettina, standing in front of the mirror with a brush in her hand, bent over at the waist and pulling it through hair that was like shimmering gold in the sunlight. He propped himself up on his elbow and watched her. He had known many beautiful women in his life. Dark ones, fair ones, women with intriguing mixtures of blood heritage. But he had never met a woman quite as beautiful as Bettina Bacheller. She was like a gift of nature, unsullied, naturally sensuous, a bright, golden spot in a life that for him had been mostly gunmetal gray.

And last night...last night had been even better than his fantasies. She had been everything and more that he imagined she would be. His nerve endings were still electrified by what they had shared. The rhythm of the train, she had claimed—embarrassed, maybe, that she had been so bold with her physical desires. But it was

A Siren's Lure 183

more than the train; he knew that for sure. The rhythm was in her, deep inside her woman's heart and body.

It was going to be torture to say good-bye to her. But, of course, that was exactly what he would have to do. His life was made up of endless comings and goings from place to place. Of running. That was no life for someone like her. She was the kind of woman who needed to be drenched in the love and attention of a man, secure in society and with a circle of friends. She claimed to be tired of the party scene, yet that was exactly where she would fit in best. She needed a man who had a solid position and a steady life. She didn't need a man like him.

But how was he going to walk away?

Bettina stood up and flipped her hair back, catching his reflection in the mirror. She examined his hair-roughened face for a moment before turning to him. "Good morning." Her smile was almost shy as her eyes automatically traveled down his body. The sheet covered his lower half; from the waist up, he was bare and solid, his skin bronze and inviting. "We're almost to Reggio di Calabria," she said a little breathlessly. "I guess from there we take the train ferry to Messina."

His gaze flicked to the window and he swung his long legs off the bed, slipping into his underwear. He got up and came to stand behind her. She was facing the mirror and watched him wrap his arms around her and kiss her temple. At the touch of his mustache and warm mouth against her skin, she closed her eyes instinctively and leaned back against him.

The knock at the door broke the hypnotic moment. John glanced at her in surprise.

184 *A Siren's Lure*

She grimaced. "I ordered us some breakfast."

His mouth dropped to her neck and he nibbled the soft flesh there. "You did, huh?"

She sighed and tilted her head farther back, giving him clear access to her neck. "Regrettably so."

The knock came again, and Erickson grumbled something in reply. He stepped back and picked up his pants off the floor. Once they were on and fastened, he opened the door and took the tray of food.

"How far are we from the station?" he asked the porter.

"Twenty minutes."

He closed the door and set the tray on the fold-down table, then let out a ragged sigh. Bettina was standing perfectly still, watching him.

"How many minutes did he say?"

"Twenty."

They stared at each other from across the small compartment. Finally, her mouth tilted upward in a provocative smile. "I guess we don't have time to eat, then."

In two strides he was in front of her, grasping the back of her neck and drawing her near. His mouth lowered ever so slowly to hers, preparing to satisfy a hunger that had nothing to do with food. "I guess not."

"QUESTIONING? They took you to the police station?"

"It's okay, Jerry. I wasn't there that long."

"I knew I shouldn't have let you do this. It was stupid of me. I should have talked you into staying home. I—"

A Siren's Lure 185

"Jerry, I'm fine, I really am."

"You are not fine, Bettina. You were supposed to be in Amalfi, not Sicily. And how did you get the Interpol investigator to let you go anyway?"

Bettina glanced across the lobby of the hotel to see if John had come back from renting a car. She wanted to be off the phone before he returned. "Erickson did it."

"How?"

"He, ah, well, he pretended to be with the American embassy in Rome."

"Oh, Lord! Dammit, Bettina, do you know what kind of trouble you two could be in? Do you have any idea? Why, they're probably hot on your tail right now, just waiting to lock you in a cage and throw away the key."

"Then we'll just have to run faster, won't we?" She laughed.

"You are not taking this very seriously. I'm worried."

"As a matter of fact, I am having fun."

"Fun!"

"Well, it's exciting. It's been a little hair-raising at times, I admit. But still..."

"Whom else have you run into?"

"What do you mean?" she asked innocently, knowing full well what he was asking and where his question could lead.

His tone was authoritative now. "I want to hear what other hair-raising incidences you've had, Bettina."

186 *A Siren's Lure*

She checked the lobby once again. "I'm not sure I should tell you if you're going to go all starchy on me."

"I won't go starchy. I'll stay perfectly calm. Now, tell me."

"Well, some insurance investigator who's after Daddy caught up with me yesterday."

"Where?"

"On the train to Sicily."

"Where was Erickson?"

"He was getting our bags. And I was in our sleep— I was in our compartment when Alvin Bilgeworth barged in. Oh, he was awful, Jerry! He's the most disgusting man!"

"What did he do?"

"Nothing. Erickson got there in time."

"Oh, cripes! That's it," Jerry snapped. "I'm coming over."

"What? Don't be ridiculous, Jerry. You promised you'd stay calm."

"Okay, I lied. I'm taking a plane tomorrow to Rome. I want to meet you there in two days."

Her voice grew indignant. "We will get there when we get there, Jerry. We are very close to Daddy, and I'm not going to give up now."

"Erickson has got you on some wild-goose chase, Bettina, and you are going to get hurt. I want you out of it. Now."

"I really don't think you have too much to say about it, Jerry. I'm not giving up."

He was silent as he assessed her clearly obstinate message. "So you're determined to keep going."

"Yes."

A Siren's Lure

187

"I'm still coming over to Rome."

"Fine. Do whatever you like." She knew she was being snippish and she hated the sound of it in her voice, but she was not going to let Jerry's paranoia disrupt everything that she and John had done so far.

"How is Erickson?" he asked.

This time, the silence was hers. He asked again, and she finally had to answer. "He's, ah..." She sighed audibly through the overseas line. "Jerry, I don't know how much longer I can deceive him and keep from telling him about you and our—our arrangment. I'm just not sure that I can lead him into your trap. I'm being unfair. I'm being...unfaithful."

"Unfaithful?" The stillness on the phone was like a deafening roar in her ears. When Jerry spoke at last, his voice had gone limp and dry. "What is that supposed to mean? Bettina, what has happened?"

"Everything."

She could hear his breath as he slowly expelled it. She could almost see the anguish in his face. "Don't fall for him, Bettina. You're going to be making a big, big mistake. Erickson has never made emotional commitments. In his line of work he couldn't. People...women were there only for the moment."

"Maybe you don't know him very well."

"Maybe you don't, either," Jerry growled. "Now listen to me, Bettina. I realize you're going to persist in finding your father. But I'm still coming to Rome. I'll stay at the Bernini and I'll wait to hear from you. We have a deal, and I expect you to follow through with it. You owe me."

"What—what are you going to do to him...once I bring him to you."

188   *A Siren's Lure*

"Let me worry about that, Bettina. You just fulfill your promise to me, okay?"

Fulfill your promise, fulfill your promise. She hung up the phone and stared broodingly at the tiled lobby floor. What was she going to do? How could she trick John like this? And yet, Jerry was her oldest and dearest friend. If it hadn't been for him, she wouldn't have gotten this close to her father. She had promised that she would help him get Erickson if he helped her locate her father. She couldn't back out on Jerry now. Could she?

THE CAR THEY RENTED in Messina was even smaller than the one they had rented in Naples, a blue Fiat that had water damage. The carpet and upholstery smelled so badly, Bettina thought she would gag. "Do you suppose they dredged this up from the bottom of the bay?"

Erickson didn't answer. Instead, he glanced toward her with a cautiously tight expression. "Whom were you talking to on the phone back there?"

Her body flinched and her eyes widened in fear and surprise. He had been in the car-rental office while she waited in the hotel lobby, and she had been watching for him the whole time she was on the phone. She had been so positive that he hadn't seen her.

"Oh...it was a—a friend back home. She's been ill and I was worried about her. I—I had promised her that I would call and see how she was doing."

His eyes left the road again to center on her face, and it was obvious he was having trouble swallowing her explanation. "So how is she?" he asked in a tone that was flat and expressionless.

A Siren's Lure 189

"She's...much better. Fine, really."

He had the brown contacts on again and was observing her so closely Bettina was beginning to squirm like a bug on a pin. She could feel a thin line of perspiration form on her upper lip and prayed that he wouldn't notice. But from the way those deep, brown eyes were drilling into her, she was sure he had missed nothing. His silence was more telling than any open accusation would have been.

The day was warm, the sky a light blue with wisps of pale clouds that hung above the mountaintops. The bare iron-gray peaks were still capped with snow, but the meadows leading up to them were lush and covered with a profusion of wildflowers. To the north, the Aeolian islands were barely visible.

Erickson glanced over at Bettina. She was staring thoughtfully out the window. "What are you thinking about?" he asked.

She turned toward him. If only she could tell him. If only she could just blurt everything out, he would know the truth and she could breathe easier. But she couldn't make the words come out, and so the knot of self-doubt continued to stick like a hard lump in the back of her throat and chest. "I'm scared," she whispered softly.

"I won't let you get hurt."

"I'm not afraid for my safety, John. I'm afraid of— of so many things. I'm worried about what will happen to my father. I'm scared to death to see him again." She closed her eyes as the pain washed over her. "The father I remember wasn't a criminal. He was a warm, loving, kind man. How am I supposed to react to him? What can I possibly say?"

190 *A Siren's Lure*

He frowned, feeling suddenly powerless to protect her from all the emotional harm that could come to her. He had always been a man with all the answers, with all the tactical moves. But with this woman's heart and soul, he was at a complete loss. He didn't know what to do.

He finally shrugged. "I'd say wait until the time comes and then let the moment and—and your heart dictate what you say and do."

She studied his profile intently. Those fertile brown eyes hid the true color beneath them. The hair was dyed almost black; the mustache was soft and thick. Nothing about his face was real, yet he was the most real person, the most complete and honest man she had ever known. And she couldn't tell Erickson that what frightened her more than her father's safety, more than her hoped-for meeting with him, more than anything else, was this arrangement she had with Jerry, this cold, calculating trap into which she had promised to lead him—the man she loved. What frightened her the most—and for the first time in her life—was her own conscience. Bettina Bacheller was scared to death of herself.

She cleared her throat. "So what do we do first? How do we go about finding him? I mean, I have no idea how one does this sort of thing. Are there special rules or guidelines?"

He maneuvered the car around the curves of the coastal road and kept an instinctive eye on the rear-view mirror. "We'll look over the town, get a feel for it, ask a few questions. But I especially want to find out where this guy Parigi lives. Then we can stake out his house, get to know his schedule—when he might

A Siren's Lure 191

be home, when not. Let's hope we can find your father before he shows up at Parigi's."

"And if we don't?"

His silence crawled over her skin and tightened around her waist like a band of cold steel.

Finally, he looked over at her and spoke in a tightly controlled voice. "Then we play a new game."

Bettina closed her eyes and leaned her head back against the seat. A new game. Her life had been a series of them, and she wondered now if and when the games would ever end.

Chapter Thirteen

The door of the coast house they had rented was open to the night breeze. At the base of an immense rock and perched on a spur that jutted into the sea, the little house was isolated from the rest of the small town. Bettina listened to the lapping sound of water slapping against the rocks below the terrace. There was no moon tonight, and only a crescent band of stars was framed by the cottage door.

Erickson was sitting on the edge of the bed, his forearms resting on his knees, a cigarette dangling from his fingers. His head was bent low, and she had to strain to hear him. "I was squeezed into the shadows of the hallway," he was saying. "I was trying to stay low against a heavy piece of furniture that was lined up along the wall. Winston and the colonel were in the next room."

"This colonel was..."

"Colonel Muro, the country's military leader." He paused for a moment as the memory collected itself. "I could hear Winston's laugh. And their glasses toasting each other. And then I heard the colonel asking about me. Winston assured him that I had been

A Siren's Lure 193

taken care of and that they didn't need to worry about me anymore." Erickson snorted derisively and took a deep drag of the cigarette.

"You mean they thought you had been killed—by the firing squad?"

He nodded slowly. "Then they started talking about the air strike. Turns out Winston had given the ground troops sufficient warning so that they were all prepared. The air assault was a miserable failure, thanks to that son of a bitch. The strike force had been counting on the element of surprise. When those guys realized they didn't have that, they weren't stupid enough to carry on with the mission."

Bettina was sitting on her knees beside him, her fingers resting lightly in his hair. She bent her head and planted a gentle kiss on the back of his neck. "But how on earth did you get away from the firing squad in the first place?"

"When the first squadron flew in, the ground troops were ready for them. But still, the planes caused enough of a commotion to shift attention away from me. These two soldiers had hold of my arms and pushed me against this wall."

Bettina closed her eyes and lowered her forehead to his shoulders. The thought of him—this man she had only moments before made love to—being led before a firing squad filled her with a terror that clutched her insides in a death grip.

"Anyway, when I heard the roar of the planes and felt them let go of my arms, something—instinct, I guess—made me run. I figured if I was shot running away, that would be no worse than being shot head-

194 *A Siren's Lure*

on. So I freed my hands, ripped off the blindfold and took the chance.''

Relief washed through her as though she were watching the action unfold, as though she were there with him in his memory. ''What I really don't understand,'' she said, ''is why you went back to the colonel's house.''

John lifted his head and smoked for a minute in silence. She sat beside him, patiently waiting. ''Keep in mind,'' he said, focusing his gaze on the darkness beyond the door, seeing things in the past that she could only imagine. ''Keep in mind that I didn't realize at this point that Winston was a double agent. All I knew was that I had been unlucky enough to be captured. I was down there to do a job, and I couldn't walk away until it was finished. I had to get the documents.''

''What were these documents?''

His eyes slid like liquid over her face. ''They were contracts—arms contracts with...with another country.'' He looked back toward the door, and she decided to let the matter drop. He had obviously told her all he was going to about the papers.

''So you got back to the house...''

''Yeah, and I was standing in the hallway behind this big thing—it was one of those old-fashioned chifforobes, I think. Winston and the colonel were in the next room, and down at the end of the hallway was where I wanted to go. The documents I wanted were in an old steamer trunk in that room. After I heard the colonel thanking Winston for his help with the air assault, I thought that all I had to do was slip down the hall and get the documents and I could be out of the country and back to the States before Winston ever

A Siren's Lure 195

knew what happened. But then..." He stared ahead, his profile grim, remembering a pain and an anger that she couldn't share. He took a final drag on the cigarette, then squashed it out in the ashtray on the floor.

She leaned over and kissed his temple, hoping to soften the hard lines of his face. He closed his eyes and placed his hand on her thigh. His thumb stroked slow circles on her flesh while he talked.

"I heard the colonel ask what kind of backlash his country could expect over my demise." Erickson chuckled low in his throat, but the sound was totally devoid of humor. "He had nothing to worry about, Winston told him. The seeds had apparently been planted, for by then I was suspected of handing over sensitive material to the Russians. Winston had made sure the agency knew I was working both sides of the fence."

"You were framed!" Bettina cried, hating Winston with an intensity she had never before experienced toward anyone. She hadn't even known the man, but she hated him for the torment he had caused John.

Erickson merely chuckled in a self-mocking way. "You might say that. He even told the colonel that if I had returned to the States, I wouldn't have lived for one day there." John looked over at her. "And he was right."

"But you could have told everyone the truth once you got home," she insisted. "You could have explained what happened."

He lifted his hand from her thigh and pulled a strand of hair over her shoulder. "You are a lovely, lovely lady, Bettina Bacheller, but you are very naive. Major Winston was not only my superior, he was a

196 *A Siren's Lure*

highly respected officer who had enough medals to fill a small vault. He was to be promoted to colonel any day. I was a captain and...well, let's just say I had never been the spit-and-polish type. I was good at what I did and the military was able to use me, but I was sort of a renegade. I didn't do things by the book; I didn't follow the proper channels.'' He shrugged. ''I rubbed a lot of people the wrong way. Now, you tell me whom you think they would have listened to—this top-brass war hero or a misfit commando like me? And believe me, I knew how double agents were handled. I had seen it all before. No one would bother to question the validity of Winston's charges. The agency would just take care of the problem. If they had let me live, it would have been in a cage for the rest of my life. No...I—I couldn't take the risk. I could not handle being confined, Bettina...even for a day.''

''So that was when you decided to run?''

There was a tight wave of silence between them. ''No,'' he finally said, looking directly at her. ''That was when I decided to kill Winston.''

She couldn't control the sharp intake of her breath. It was automatic, instinctive. People—at least the people she had known—didn't stand around at cocktail parties and talk of murder in such a calm, matter-of-fact manner.

She evened out her breath and watched him lean back with his elbows resting on the mattress. ''But first,'' he continued, ''I knew I had to get the documents. I was going to take care of Winston later. I made it down to the room at the end of the hall, picked the lock on the trunk and got the papers. But I found a little bonus in the process. There was a false bottom

A Siren's Lure

in the trunk, and beneath it was a box of jewels—diamonds, emeralds, a sizable collection of pretty fine stuff. So I stuffed the jewels into the pockets of my jeans. I had lost my shirt when I ran from the soldiers, but I crammed in as many jewels as I could into my pants.''

His eyes narrowed, forming tiny creases at the corners as he stared across the dark room. Only the light in the kitchen was on; it sent a yellow beam slanting across the wood floor. ''You know,'' he said, ''at the time I thought it was so odd that the house wasn't under better guard. But after I understood that they were all prepared for the invasion, I realized there was no need. They were confident that nothing would happen. Anyway, I saw Winston leave through the front door, so I slipped out the back and ran across the lawn toward this iron fence at the rear of the grounds. I could hear the dogs barking in the distance, but they didn't seem very close, so I just kept going. I had hoisted myself over the fence and was just climbing down to the other side when I heard the explosion.''

Jerry had told her that Winston's car was blown up that night, but she couldn't let Erickson know that. She wanted to, but she couldn't. ''What was it?'' she asked, hating herself for the lies and deceptions that she kept piling up, one on top of the other.

''Winston's car.'' He sneered in a low and ugly tone. ''The colonel's people saved me the trouble. They took care of him for me. I had run through the cover of the trees, and no one had yet made it to the scene of the explosion. But I could hear the sounds of voices, agitated and loud, and footsteps pounding on the dirt

198 *A Siren's Lure*

road. I knew it was only a matter of seconds until a hundred people showed up.''

He was quiet for so long, she finally had to ask. ''What did you do then?''

He looked over at her, studying her young innocence, wondering how truthful he should be with her. ''I had been in a lot of battles,'' he said quietly. ''A lot of tense political situations, Bettina. I had learned to use my instincts. So I did what I thought I had to do to survive.''

She was staring at him both intrigued and unnerved by a code of ethics she could not understand.

''Winston had an escort with him, driving the car. He had been thrown after the explosion and was still alive, but just barely. He would never have made it to a hospital. I took out the false passport I was carrying and switched it with his wallet and identification.''

''But wouldn't someone have recognized that man and known it wasn't you? If he was thrown from the car, he obviously wasn't...'' She stopped in stunned horror when she noticed the icy glaze that had crept into John's face. The hard, fixed expression in his eyes told her that he no longer saw the room they were in. He was looking right through it, beyond it to another time and place.

He began speaking even more quietly, almost hypnotically, his eyes directed at the floor in front of him, his voice a dull, listless monotone. ''A portion of the flaming car blew off and landed beside him. I could have kicked it away. I didn't.''

Bettina's eyes closed, and she felt something bitter rising in the back of her throat. Jerry had said it all before. *He was a soldier, Bettina. In his line of work,*

A Siren's Lure **199**

bodies were a dime a dozen. He was trying to save his own hide....

It was several agonizingly long minutes before she could find the courage to speak. When she did, her voice was not much more above a whisper. "So...you took the new identity and the jewels and—and you ran."

He sat up once again and rested his arms on his legs. "I wasn't sure how tight a frame Winston had built around me at the agency. All I knew was that I couldn't take the chance of going back. If Winston had convinced the military that I was the double agent, I would have either been...deleted from the rank and file or locked away forever. On Winton's say alone, I would have been in deep trouble. And that doesn't count my being AWOL for five years. I had no idea where I would go or what would happen next. All I knew was I had to keep running. I couldn't turn back. And I couldn't go home." His hands came up to cradle his head, his elbows digging into his thighs. "I've never told anyone about it before."

She wrapped her arm around his broad, rock-hard shoulders and pressed her mouth gently against the dark hair at the base of his neck, her lips gliding across to his ear. "How could you have held it all in for so long?" she whispered. "How could you have kept it all to yourself?"

He let his hands drop to the mattress and looked at her steadily. "I never trusted anyone before."

Her breath caught in her throat and tears began to well up.

Trust. She was the only one he had trusted enough. And she was the one who had promised to betray him.

The back of her throat was clogged with the painful realization of what she had been doing. She had duped him all along, leading him straight into a trap. She was helping to take the only thing in life he had left—his freedom. She couldn't do that to him. She just couldn't. Somehow, she would find a way to stop it from happening. But how could she prevent it without letting him know that she had deceived him all along?

"You make me realize all the things I've missed," he said, reaching around her and pulling her close. "I've been running all my life, it seems, and now—that I've met you, I realize that I don't want to run anymore."

Her eyes were filled with tears when she lifted them to his face, but he didn't see the guilt and pain in them. He saw only the hope, the possibilities of what they could do and be together. Yet he had to dash that hope in both of them before it was too late.

"But...I can't stop. You do realize that."

She climbed off the bed and knelt in front of him, running her hands along the tops of his thighs. "We could go to—to that land at the end of the earth," she whispered tearfully. "No one would bother us there." She knew now how much she loved this man, knew she would run with him for the rest of their lives. She would do whatever it took to be with him.

He looped his arms around her and wedged her between his legs, his hands moving up to rest against the sides of her face. "I've been alone too long, Bettina. Doing things my way, picking up and taking off whenever I felt the need to go."

"I could go with you!" she cried, earnestly believing it.

He smiled gently and shook his head. "No, you couldn't. I mean, who knows, maybe I'll fight in another war somewhere down the line."

She swallowed hard. "A—a mercenary?"

"I was trained as a commando, Bettina. It's what I do best. I've been a thief and I do that very well, too. All the things I do best are not what makes for a good provider." The pressure of his hands against her face increased, and his fingers slid beneath her hair. "You need a good man, Bettina, a good husband and a provider. You don't need a war-hardened soldier on the run. You don't need me. And—" He broke off and drew her face into the hollow of his neck, resting his chin on the top of her head. "And I don't need you."

The words echoed painfully through the chambers of her mind, filling her body with a sharp, biting ache that she knew would never go away. How could she let this man simply disappear from her life? Once he was gone, she would never find him again. He would make sure of it.

"Just walk away from each other," she murmured dully against his neck. She pulled back and regarded him thoughtfully. "Can you look at me and do that?"

He angled his eyes away from her, not wanting to take any chances. "Yes."

"You make it sound very simple." She laid her palms flat against the sides of his jaw and forced him to look at her. "You make it sound so cut-and-dried."

The muscle in his cheek jumped, and then he purposely hardened his jaw. "It is, Bettina. You just have to accept it."

"And if I can't?" She saw him swallow and watched the pounding of the pulse in his neck. Her eyes fixed on his, but he was looking through her, refusing to see her.

When he spoke, his voice was clear and dry and very certain. "You have no choice."

Chapter Fourteen

Rain fell in a fine mist on the stone street, leaving it slick and shiny. The sky was lead gray, as if the rain would go on forever, and the air was thick with the smell of fish. The town huddled sleepily under the wetness of the day, its wrought-iron balconies empty of the usual assortment of clothes hung out to dry. Shopkeepers stood idly in their doorways, hoping for a break in the weather.

Bettina hurried out of the small store with a sack of food and ran through the rain to the car. She climbed into the front seat and quickly closed the door, shivering from the wet cold. Erickson reached over and peered into the sack. "Bread, cheese, wine...what's this?"

She grimaced at the packet of meat he was holding. "They said it was ham, but...I don't know."

"We're better off not knowing," he said, tossing it back into the bag.

"I've got some napkins and a corkscrew and...I think I've got everything we'll need."

He turned the key, and the engine began to hum. "Good, because there's nothing worse than a stakeout without food."

204 *A Siren's Lure*

Through the rhythmic tick of the windshield wipers, she listened carefully to his tone of voice, as she had been listening to it all day, trying to read its message. Like hers, it was light and inconsequential; he was full of jokes and easy laughter. But the bantering between them was forced, and they both knew it. Last night had changed everything.

She stared blankly at the fine sheet of rain that was falling; she felt as if one of them had some sort of terminal illness and was going to die soon. Of course, she knew that it was she who would suffer the most. Erickson was a man. He had been on the move for all his adult life. He would just walk away, leaving her behind to pick up the pieces.

She loved him. Even though she had not said those exact words to him, he had to know it. Hadn't she shown him in a hundred small ways? And yet, in the end, he was still going to walk away. She was still going to lose him.

He shifted the car into drive and pulled away from the curb. At that precise moment, Bettina had been staring through the windshield at an old man in a woolen coat who crouched against a darkened doorway. She had been thinking about Erickson and feeling miserably sorry for herself when she saw the cane. It was a creamy white cane with a gold-tipped handle—right there in the middle of the narrow rainsoaked sidewalk. Ancient buildings that looked as if they were propping one another up bordered the winding street, blocking light even on the sunniest of days. Still, something had struck the tip of the cane, causing it to sparkle and catch her attention.

A Siren's Lure 205

By chance Stephen Bacheller had pivoted and was facing their direction, and Bettina had her first view of her father in seven years. But a second later, he had swung back the other way and hurried down the street, his collar pulled up protectively around his neck.

"Oh, my God, John! It's him!" She yanked open the car door and started to climb out, but Erickson grabbed her arm and held her back. "What are you doing!" she cried. "I've got to go to him!"

"Take a look behind him, Bettina."

She followed his line of vision and saw two men dash out of the same building from which her father had emerged only seconds before. She caught a glimpse of one of the men's faces. It was thin and hard and impatient. Not a man who would listen to reason. They were both young, probably in their late twenties. Dressed in jeans and expensive leather jackets, they plunged through the puddles, heading straight for her father.

Bacheller stopped and turned around. Seeing the men behind him, he spun back and dove into the road, splashing through the huge puddle of water as he ran toward the end of the block. The two younger men hesitated, but only for a second, before reaching into their jackets and drawing out pistols.

"John! We have to help him!" Bettina urged.

Before her cry was complete, Erickson was out of the car. She yanked open the door on her side and jumped out after him. He was already halfway down the street.

The mist was blowing in from the sea, and within minutes, Bettina was chilled to the bone. Her cardigan sweater was inadequate cover for this weather, but

206 *A Siren's Lure*

she thought only of the driving need to reach her father. The smells of fish and garlic mingled in the moist air and clung to her skin and hair as she ran. Her canvas shoes were soaked, and her chest hurt from the fear and the cold.

She rounded the corner and saw that Erickson had crossed the street and was heading down a steep, stone stairway that led to the beach, which was gray and empty now.

She ran faster, terrified by the thought of those guns the two men had drawn. She had heard no shots...yet. But her nerves were stretched taut with the expectation of that sound—the ear-shattering burst of gunshots splitting the air in two—and with the unthinkable sight of her father crumpling to the ground. She had come so close. So close. She could not bear the thought of anything happening to him now. It would be the cruelest irony of all.

Breathless and soaked, she caught up with Erickson. He had stopped on the stairway and was looking back toward the street. She reached out and clutched his arm, too tired to speak.

He glanced down at her pale, wet face, then immediately shifted his gaze to the street. "Look," he said, breathing rapidly and wiping away the drops of water from his face, "there he goes. Somehow...he made it to his car."

She looked around just as a light blue Mercedes sped by. Behind the wheel was her father. Waving her arms frantically in the air, she tried to signal him, to make him notice her standing there in the rain. But the car never slowed at all.

She dropped her arms to her sides and shivered. Well, at least he had made it. He had gotten safely away from the men who were after him. But where was he going?

Bettina leaned against the strong support of Erickson's body. His shirt was damp, and she breathed in the scent of the flannel material mixed with his own manly smell. His arm came around her and held her close. "It's okay, honey," he said, low and warm against the top of her head. "We'll find him again."

She looked up at John. "Where do you think he's going? And those men...were they Interpol?"

"Not by the looks of them."

"You mean...Mafia?"

"More than likely. Probably Parigi's men."

"Then that would mean he has already stolen the angels."

Erickson expelled a deep breath. "It sure as hell looks that way." He glanced down quickly when he felt her clutch his arm again. She was focusing on the foot of the stairs, so he swung his gaze in that direction. The two men wearing the leather jackets were walking back up from the beach. Their guns were no longer in their hands, and the impatience in their faces had burned down to a smoldering anger.

Bettina held her breath and clung tightly to Erickson's arm as the men passed by, cursing and mumbling between clenched teeth.

Erickson grabbed her and pulled her up the stairway and toward the car. "Come on," he commanded. "We've got to hurry."

"Why? What's happened?"

"He's on his way to Monreale."

"Are you sure?"

His eyes narrowed on the two men who had cut off down a narrow alleyway, heading up toward the cen-

208 *A Siren's Lure*

ter of town. "No, but from what I could hear, those two guys seemed to be pretty sure. So," he concluded, opening the car door for her, "we'll go back to the cottage, get our things and then head that way."

"We're always right behind him," she lamented. "Always behind."

Erickson leaned down through the doorway and gently wiped away some droplets of water on her face. "We're going to catch up with him, Bettina. I promise you that."

She stared up at him, at the water streaming down his wet hair. "Thank you," she said.

His brows drew together in puzzlement. "For what?"

She looked beyond the Italian facade he wore and saw the man beneath. Her smile was radiant. "For everything. For not running from me when I first told you why I had come to Capri. For not tossing me over the cliff. For not leaving me in Pompeii when you know you should have. For giving me hope."

Had she professed an undying love and need for him, he would have felt no stronger emotions than he did in that moment. She needed him. She wanted him as a man and as her protector and defender. And he knew he would defy all of the ancient gods' warnings to be at her side, for however short a time; to listen to her songs, however dangerous or destructive they were; and to lie in her arms, no matter how hard it would be to leave them.

THE SKY HAD CLEARED, and the mountains were brilliant with the colors of the wildflowers, the air heavy with their intoxicating scent. From Monreale, the view over the hillsides was of chestnut and ash trees, a car-

A Siren's Lure 209

pet of green broken by the torrential rivers that fed down into the ever-present orange and lemon groves. Between these, nestled beige villas with red-tiled roofs and the winding road that sliced its way down from the mountain into Palermo.

The two men walked slowly, side by side, along the arcade of the cloister. Its Moorish heritage was evident in its arches of Arab-Byzantine blend, supported by stone columns the color of Marsala wine, carved with medieval sculptures and inlaid with rich-colored mosaics. In the center of the lesser quadrangle, a graceful column served as the shaft of the fountain, which spurted cool, clear water into a tile bowl at its base. The afternoon light cast long shadows across the cloister gardens and under the shelter of the arcade.

"It has been a long road for you, signore. But you have done remarkably well."

Stephen Bacheller shifted the cane to his other hand. "That remains to be seen."

"At least you have completed the matter at hand. And for that, I am very grateful. The entire staff of the cathedral will be grateful. You have taken many risks for this."

Bacheller shrugged. "You have paid me well for my time and trouble."

"Ah, yes, but you could have sold these for a much higher price to other buyers, other collectors."

"I know that."

The man studied Stephen as they walked. "You have a big heart and soul."

"No, I'm just getting soft in my old age, that's all."

"Whatever it is, I am grateful. These angels will go into the Treasury, the crown perhaps into the right wing of the transept with the marble tombs of Wil-

210 *A Siren's Lure*

liam I and William II. And the mosaic...that beautiful work of art will go into the Chapel of the Crucified Christ. This is where they belong. It is time they took their rightful place among the treasures of Monreale.'' The man sighed, satisfied that everything was where it belonged. "And where will you go now? Ah, I must not ask that."

Stephen chuckled lightly, but his eyes were creased with worry. Right now, he was wondering the same thing. Where would he go? He knew that Antonio Parigi had sent his dogs after him and that they would be waiting outside in the square...or perhaps even now they were slinking through the rooms of the cathedral, watching his every move, waiting for the right moment to put a bullet through his heart. No, that would be too easy, much too quick. They would no doubt find a much slower and more painful way for him to die.

"My first task is to get back to my car," he said.

"Did you leave it in the square?"

"Yes."

"Then follow me. We will go through the Benedictine monastery and then through the royal palace. It is a roundabout way to go, but it may be safer."

As they walked, Stephen tried to plan out his every move. He had several in mind, but he was realistic enough to expect that Parigi's men would anticipate his every step. No matter what he did or which way he decided to go, they would have him. Only a miracle could help him now.

At the bronze door of the palace, he said good-bye to the man and slipped out into the late-afternoon sun of the town square.

A Siren's Lure 211

SQUINTING HIS EYES into the sun, Erickson saw him first. Bettina spotted him only a few seconds later and had to be physically restrained once again from jumping out of the car.

"I'm not going to lose him again!" she insisted. "Let me go!"

"Bettina, take a look around the square. Do you see those two men over there in the gray suits?"

"Yes. Mafia?"

"Interpol. Those three next to the black Mercedes limo are probably Parigi's men. You won't be doing your father any favors by running after him."

"What are we going to do?" she cried frantically, watching the men close in on her father. "We've got to help him! I can't stand any more of this!"

Erickson was only too well aware of the dangerous situation that Bacheller was in, and he knew that if he was going to help, he had to act fast. But first of all, he had to get Bettina out of there. He grabbed her arms and forced her to look at him. "Listen to me very, very carefully. I'm going to get out of the car with my duffel bag, and I want you to drive to Palermo."

"Palermo! But—but—"

"There is no time to argue, Bettina," he snapped, giving her a hard shake. "Now listen to me and do as I say. Your father is in big trouble. And if you want me to help him, you've got to be away from here. Besides, I need you in Palermo."

"Why?" she asked weakly, almost in tears again.

"I want you to go to the dock and buy three tickets on the overnight steamer to Naples. Then go to the airport and wait in the car—someplace where you can

212 *A Siren's Lure*

see us drive up. I don't know whether we'll be in your father's Mercedes or what, but we'll see you."

"Why the airport if we're going on a boat?"

"We need a diversion. I'm hoping that will provide it. I won't know for sure until we get there. But I want you to do that." He stared at her hard, trying to make sure she understood. "Go now, okay?" He climbed out of the car.

She scooted over behind the steering wheel, her face pale and full of worry about what was going to happen to all of them. "You'll be careful?" she asked him through the open window.

"I'll take good care of him, Bettina."

She felt the tears well up in her eyes and thought she would choke on her fear. "I wasn't talking about him. I was talking about you."

He looked down at her and drew in a deep breath. His hand brushed lightly against her face and hair, and his voice was rough with emotion. "I will.... Now go."

With his eyes shaded against the setting sun, he watched her back the Fiat around and drive away from the square and down the side of the mountain.

Chapter Fifteen

Bettina kept her foot weighted on the gas pedal, driving too fast along a road that snaked down from the mountains and wound through fields of wildflowers. The blues and yellows and reds of the hillsides were rich and fragrant; the sea to the right was a bright blue under the sun. It was a paradise, but Bettina had no time or inclination to notice it, much less enjoy it. The panorama passed by her in a blur, as merely another mile, another stretch of road, before she reached her destination. It was only five miles to Palermo, but they were the longest five miles of her life.

She tried to concentrate on the specific act of getting there and buying the tickets. But peripheral images kept forcing their way into her consciousness. There was her father, stepping from the shadows of the palace into the patch of sunlight in the town square. There were the two men in jeans and leather jackets, leaning against a black Mercedes. There were the gray-suited men. There was Erickson's hard profile as he took in the scene and made a snap decision. Bettina had come so close to finding her father, she didn't want to lose him now; not this way. She didn't approve of what he was doing, but she didn't want him to die at the hands of other men. She had gotten used to the idea that he had died as a result of a tragic accident on one of his adventurous romps through the Himalayas. That was the way he would want to go, not in this brutal, murderous manner.

And then there was John. Her eyes closed briefly and her hands gripped the wheel more tightly. If anything happened to him...

She had gotten him involved in this in the first place. He had been content, living peacefully and in seclusion in his little white house perched high on the cliff, with the orange and lemon groves flanking one side, a small vineyard on the other and the whole blue sea beyond. She had taken him away from it all. She had disrupted his life and brought new fears and new dangers into it. Now he was worried about staying alive and out of jail.

She checked the road sign ahead. Palermo was only three more miles. She was almost there. She had to concentrate on what she was supposed to do. *Keep your mind on track, Bettina, and stop thinking about all the other possibilities.* All of the "what ifs."

She had never thought about them before this trip to Europe, so why were they constantly on her mind now? All her life, she had dealt only with the present, with the here and now. She had never worried about the consequences of her actions, never looked ahead much to the future, never bothered to reflect on her past. "Live for the moment" had been her motto. But now that she looked back on it, she realized she had never done anything of value. Not once. Where had

A Siren's Lure 215

she been all those years? Where was she going? It had never mattered in the least until now.

And, too, she had always been alone. A solitary floater, moving like a weightless feather with the currents of air. Her father was the only person who had ever mattered in her life. He was the only one she had ever had, and she hadn't had him very often. And that had determined her relationships with everyone else. Her relationships with both men and women had been shallow for the most part, never deep enough for her to be hurt if they moved on or left her for another. Floating toward someone, then flitting off on the next current of air had also never mattered in the least until now.

Erickson had changed everything.

His life had been so different from hers. He had always been on the move, always forging a path through troubled waters, always knowing where he was going, where he had been, where he had to be next. Unlike her, he had not simply floated through life. He had planned strategies, charted maneuvers, made goals. Yes, he had been a thief and a ruthless soldier and—perhaps on many occasions—a killer. But those things no longer mattered to her. The only thing that mattered was that she loved him.

But she had deceived him.

She wanted now to change all of that. She only hoped that it was not too late.

As soon as Bettina had driven off, Erickson dug down into his duffel bag. Pulling out a small incendiary device, he stuck it in the inside pocket of his jacket and headed toward the Mercedes limousine, parked to

216   *A Siren's Lure*

the right of the fountain. Parigi's men had moved slowly to the left, in the direction of the palace door through which Bacheller had come out. Erickson took a cigarette lighter from his pocket, lit the device, tossed it beneath the front of the car, and moved away quickly.

Within seconds, the sparks caught and smoke began to billow upward. It was just the diversion he had wanted. At the shouts of the people in the square, Parigi's men turned around, cursed loudly and ran back to the limousine. Even the two Interpol agents were lost for a few seconds in the chaos.

If Bacheller had just stayed put, Erickson could have reached him in time. But instead, when the fire had broken out, he had taken the opportunity to make a mad dash for his own car. Unfortunately, the fire had not diverted the Interpol agents long enough. They saw Bacheller making a run for it and headed straight after him.

Erickson was only a few paces behind them, dodging the crowd of tourists in the square. He ran faster, trying to catch up to the two men. Suddenly, he hurled himself forward, smashing hard into their backs. With arms flailing in a vain effort to break their falls, they lost their footing and toppled forward. John was right on top of them.

He rolled to the side and jumped up. Stephen Bacheller had turned around and was staring at him, but after a second he started his flight again. Erickson ran after him. A shot rang out from somewhere, behind him, and he looked back. Parigi's men had lost interest in their burning car and were once again in pursuit of their target. Erickson had to move faster,

A Siren's Lure 217

had to get to Bettina's father first. Another shot was fired. Screams issued from the terrifed crowd, and a chaotic mass exodus from the square began.

Erickson was right behind Bacheller now. The old man was slow; he couldn't keep up the pace. This time the gunshot was much closer, zinging past Erickson and burying itself in the wall next to him. He kicked open a side door to the cathedral, reached around Bacheller and dragged him inside. They were in the south wing transept, where a huge mosaic of Satan tempting Jesus towered over them.

"This way," Erickson commanded, pulling the old man behind him.

"Who the hell are you?" Bacheller demanded, his breath raspy and tight in his chest. He was being hustled along by a man he had never laid eyes on before.

"I'm a friend of Bettina's. Now hurry. This way." They had moved into the south apse, slipping behind the alter of the central apse. An enormous mosaic of Christ loomed above the sanctuary.

"Bettina!" her father cried, the lines around his eyes deepening. "Where...what..."

Erickson opened the door into the chapel and pushed Bacheller in front of him. He could hear the sound of running footsteps and knew that the men were still following. And they weren't too far behind, either. "I'll explain later. Let's just get you out of here. Where's your car?"

"In the square."

Erickson shook his head. "That's no good. We'll have to find another."

They quickly moved into the Treasury, where the precious antiques of the cathedral were kept: a jewel-

218   *A Siren's Lure*

encrusted pastoral staff, a wooden inlaid cupboard, gold, mosaics, priceless jewels.

"Get me out of here," Stephen mumbled. "My mouth is starting to water in this place."

They hurried through another door and found themselves in a driveway behind the cathedral. A steep drop-off cliff edged the driveway where it led down to the main road below. A priest was walking slowly from the cathedral toward the orchard at the side of the building. Stephen recognized him immediately.

"Father," he called. "Father, we need help."

The man hurried over to them with a concerned expression. "There are problems?"

"Big problems," Stephen said. "We need a car."

The man nodded. "Come this way." He led them along the rear wall of the cathedral and around the far corner until they came to an old, beat-up Volkswagen van. He took a set of keys from his robe and handed them to Bacheller.

Staring at the heap in front of them, Erickson looked dubious.

"God works in mysterious ways," the priest explained, opening the car doors for them. Bacheller got in on the passenger side.

"If you say so, Father," Erickson climbed in behind the wheel and backed the van around. Blackened exhaust spurted from the tailpipe as the vehicle headed down the drive and toward the steep, curving mountain road. In his rearview mirror, Erickson saw Parigi's men round the back of the cathedral, the guns still gripped in their hands, their eyes searching the shadows for the two men on foot. They never even noticed the van as it drove away from the cathedral.

A Siren's Lure 219

All they saw was an old priest walking slowly toward an orchard.

BETTINA WAS SITTING in her car at the Palermo airport, parked in a spot just inside the main entrance. She had checked out the grounds thoroughly and knew there was another entrance through which John and her father could come. But this one was closer to the main road. If they came the way she had, they would enter here. She would be ready for them. She would be ready for anything.

She saw a car traveling down the road, and her heart began to pound. Moments later, a car turned in and parked beside her. Bettina let out a disappointed sigh. A family of four emerged, heading for the terminal. With every automobile that had come along in the last hour, the result had been the same. Her heart began to pound again, and her hands became clammy. Her nerves were on the brink of shattering. What if they didn't show up? What if something had happened to them? What if...

Another car was approaching the airport. But it would be the same thing. She knew it. Still...

An old gray van had turned in and pulled up beside the Fiat. She stared in disbelief as Erickson climbed from behind the wheel and opened the door. Within seconds she had jumped out of the car and thrown her arms around his neck, holding him tight, her body shaking with all the fears that had been relieved by the mere sight of him. She stepped back and smiled; then her eyes swung to the other man.

Her father walked around the front of the van and stopped, staring at her from a spot no more than ten

A Siren's Lure

feet away. He was much older now. Seven years older. And shorter than she had remembered him. His hair was solid white, his face etched with fine lines. But he was her father, the man she never thought she would ever see again. He had come back from the dead. He was standing before her. He was alive.

"Daddy!" she cried, running to him and throwing her arms around him. "Oh, Daddy, you're alive! You're here!" She was crying and kissing his cheek and holding him as tightly as he was holding her. His body was still strong and vibrant, and the years fell away once his arms closed around her.

Erickson touched her shoulder lightly. "Bettina," he said, his tone almost apologetic. "We don't have time for...we have to go. Someone could have spotted us leaving Monreale."

Her father set her at arm's length and spoke in a voice that was as clear and authoritative as it had always been. "He is right, Bettina. There will be time to talk later."

Still crying and never taking her eyes off him, she reluctantly agreed. The three of them climbed into the Fiat, with Erickson driving and Stephen sitting in the back beside the sack of food and wine that Bettina had purchased earlier that day. As they drove down the road toward the dock, Bettina reached back and gripped her father's hand. Now that she had found him again, she would not let go.

Chapter Sixteen

The sway of the ship was so gentle, it was almost as if it were not moving at all. Left behind, with a smooth plane of sea between, were the soft sand beaches and the bare gray mountains of Sicily. Ahead was the mainland, a long sweeping coast of jutting cliffs, moonlit bays and tiny rocky islands that floated in the midst of the sea. Outside, the air was cold. But inside the cabin, with the full moon framed by the round porthole, the air was filled with smoke from the two men's cigars and with the noise of their animated, triumphant voices. It also echoed with the sound of three glasses clinking together in a toast.

Bettina, wearing tight jeans and one of Erickson's bulky sweaters, curled up on the bunk bed with a glass of Frascati in her hand. She listened at times with fear, excitement or pleasure as the two men related the details of their harrowing escapade. They were full of themselves, full of the stuff that made them men. And she loved it. She couldn't get enough of it. The two men she loved most on earth were with her, safe and warm and on the verge of getting happily drunk.

A Siren's Lure

But after all the tall tales, the fiery edge of their talk had burned off, leaving all of them with a warm glow. Bettina had so much to ask her father, she wasn't even sure where to begin. But with the wine warming her insides and loosening her thoughts, she said the first thing that came to mind.

"Why, Daddy?" she asked in bewilderment. "Why did you—and when did this all start?"

Erickson was sitting on the floor, his back resting against the edge of the bunk bed, the wineglass balanced on his bent knee. Bacheller leaned forward in a chair by the small fold-down table. He was holding the bottle in his hands, appearing to study the label with single-minded concentration. When he finally spoke, his voice was layered with age.

"It's never been the same for me...." He glanced over at Bettina. "Not since your mother died." He looked back at the bottle and talked to it. It was easier that way. The wine bottle didn't have eyes full of hurt and confusion looking back at him. "When I met Elizabeth, she was—she was everything I had ever wanted. She was my life. We were so much in love. And when you were born, Bettina, everything *we* wanted was there. We were a family. Life was complete."

He poured himself another glass of wine, draining the bottle. Erickson leaned over, pulled another from the sack and handed it up to him.

"After she was gone," Stephen continued, "I had my business. I had my little girl. But...nothing was the same." He looked over at Bettina, sitting so still across from him. "I loved you, you know that. But there was this emptiness...."

A Siren's Lure 223

She swallowed, holding back the tears that wanted to fall. She had been so naive, so sure that the world had revolved around her. If only she had known.

Bacheller shrugged. "So it started out as a game. I needed something to replace the void. I needed some excitement." He chuckled to himself. "I began to realize how easy—how incredibly easy—it would be for me to take advantage of my rich contacts in Europe, as well as in other parts of the world. I was always invited to wonderful parties with all of the wealthiest people. I had access to villas in France with priceless art objects, to yachts with precious cargo smuggled from the Mideast, to women's bedrooms with safes tucked neatly in the wall behind the paintings. It was a game."

Bettina glanced at Erickson. He had been watching her closely during Stephen's explanation, and now he reached out to her with his hand. She laid hers in his palm, and his strong, brown fingers closed over hers.

"And those things from Monreale?" she asked her father. "How did you get involved in that? Did you know they were stolen a long time ago from the cathedral?"

"Oh, yes, I knew that."

"What did you do with them?" She was not sure she really wanted to know. The priest from Amalfi had convinced her that their rightful place was in Monreale. She didn't want to hear that they had gone to the highest bidder.

"I returned them to the cathedral."

She stared back at him. "You mean you stole them and then gave them—"

224 *A Siren's Lure*

"Bettina," he said in a fatherly tone, "I didn't give them away. I sold them."

Her forehead drew together while she waited for his explanation.

"It's a rather long and complicated story," he said. "But the end result of it is that I met one of the benefactors of the cathedral and we struck a deal. I would steal the crown, the angels and the mosaic and sell them to a group of men who were all benefactors and curators of the cathedral and who were willing to pay my price." He stopped and took a drink of wine. "Don't look at me like that, Bettina. I'm a thief. I've been one for too many years to count. I've been through all the moral ramifications of what I do, and to be honest, I don't want to go through them with you. It's part of the reason I—I disappeared seven years ago. I thought it would be easier for you that way. Since at that time no one suspected me, all the money from the estate would be yours upon my death. And you were an adult and could make it on your own."

"Easier?" she choked out bitterly. "Easier to think my father is dead and that I'll never see him again? Easier to be alone—with no one in my life? Easier to have the government come in and take over my inheritance, my house, everything I owned? No, Daddy, you were wrong there! It wasn't easy!"

Bettina felt the pressure of Erickson's fingers increase. Her hand was warm inside his, and his head was leaning back, resting on her thigh.

Stephen saw the way they were sitting. He had noticed the little gestures between them all night, the ones that said so much without saying anything at all. He

A Siren's Lure   225

smiled to himself, satisfied with his daughter's choice. "So," he said, "what's on your agenda now?"

She shrugged. "You know, I really don't know. Now that I've found you, I—well, I guess I'm free to do whatever I want."

Erickson spoke up, his own voice full of authority. "We'll stay in Rome for a few days. We'll make it a holiday."

Bettina snatched her hand back from his as if she had just been bitten by a snake. She jumped off the bed and stood against the wall. "No!"

He frowned up at her. "What's the matter?"

"Not Rome," she answered emphatically. "You can't stay there. You've—we've got to leave the minute we dock."

His frown grew deeper, and his brown eyes narrowed on her in dark study. "Why?" he asked in a suddenly cold, even tone. His mouth was tight and controlled, in anticipation of bad news.

"Because—because it's too crowded this time of year," she said quickly. "We could go somewhere else. We could..." His eyes were so dark, so demanding of the truth, that she couldn't bear to look him in the face. She turned her back on both men and stared out the porthole.

"What is it, honey?" her father asked.

Her shoulders began to shake, and she leaned her forehead against the wall. The only sounds in the cabin were the light hum of the ship's motors and the sobs from her throat.

She heard the scrape of her father's chair and spun around, tears streaming down her face. "No, Daddy, don't." She looked at Erickson, anguish written in every line of her face and in every syllable that was uttered from her quivering lips. "You can't stay in Rome, John. Someone from—from the DIA is there to pick you up."

He didn't say a word. Neither did Bacheller. The silence in the cabin was almost deafening. And the look on John's face made Bettina's insides feel as if they were being ripped apart.

"I wanted to find my father," she whispered. "It was the only way. I made a deal—and—oh, John, please say something."

His eyes closed, and he sat still with that unfeeling mask of his firmly in place where his face should have been. Finally, after interminable minutes, he opened his eyes and stared at her. "I knew it from the beginning," he said in an even monotone. "I knew it was a trap and, like a jackass, I fell right into it. I played right into your hands." He shook his head over his own stupidity. "It's all been a ruse, hasn't it? All of it."

She was shaking her own head, but she couldn't find the words to make him understand. "Not all," she murmured.

He scowled at her. "I'll bet! So tell me—who is it at the agency?"

She swallowed hard. "Jerry McCluskey."

"McCluskey," he said with a sneer. "So you and the old desk jockey cooked up this little scheme together. Must have been fun."

"I had to find my father, John. It was the only way Jerry would tell me where you were."

Stephen's eyes went back and forth between the two of them, understanding enough to know that what had

A Siren's Lure 227

gone on between his daughter and this man was more than a professional arrangement and that now that arrangement was on the verge of collapse.

Erickson's gaze was still riveted on Bettina's face, and when he spoke again, his voice was cold. "If he knew where I was, why hasn't he picked me up before now?"

She shook her head. "I don't know. I—I'm not sure he really wanted to. But now..." She lifted her hands in a feeble gesture. "He was so insistent on coming over to Italy. He knows you weren't a double agent, John. The whole agency knows that. But still..." So much had happened in the past week of her life. She had been forced to be suspicious of everyone. She had been forced not to trust. Jerry was her friend, but then he had been Erickson's friend, too. She hated to believe that Jerry could lock Erickson away. "I have no idea what he's going to do," she murmured. "But I do know that we can't stay here. We have to take off as soon as we dock."

"We?" John snarled. "What the hell is this 'we' business? This has nothing to do with you. You've got what you wanted." He stood up and snatched his jacket from the chair, then glanced from father to daughter without trying to contain his feeling of derision. "And as you have made perfectly clear before, Bettina Bacheller always gets what she wants. So," he said, thrusting his arms into the jacket, "drink and be merry, you two."

He picked up his wineglass and in one smooth motion flung it against the wall, where it shattered in a thousand pieces. Jerking open the door, he stalked out

228   *A Siren's Lure*

into the passageway, but not before he had closed the door with a resounding slam.

The tears in Bettina's eyes were gone, and only a sharp pain was left in the hollow of her chest. Slowly she stepped to the table and sat down across from her father, dropping her head into the cradle of her arms.

Stephen reached out and rested his hand on the top of her head, impotent to find the cure for what now ailed his only child.

She finally lifted her tear-streaked face and stared at him, pain radiating out from her eyes. Her voice was a low, tortured cry as she asked, "What am I going to do, Daddy? I've made a terrible mess of my life."

THE WIND WAS BITINGLY COLD, but it felt good to him, slapping against his face, rustling through his hair as the ship skimmed across the water. The air was clear and fresh, tinged with the light odor of fish. High in the night sky, the moon cast white pools of light down on the sea.

Erickson leaned his forearms on the deck and smoked a cigarette, staring at a patch of moonlight on the rippling water. He was numb, but that feeling had not come from the temperature outside. He didn't even want to think; he just wanted to be numb.

After a while, he glanced sideways and noticed that Stephen was standing next to him. He turned his gaze back to the water, intent upon that rippling patch of moonlight.

Bacheller rested his hands on the railing and followed Erickson's gaze. "There's much to be said for being a solitary man, isn't there?"

A Siren's Lure 229

Erickson didn't answer. He had nothing to say...to anyone.

Stephen hadn't really expected an answer. From what Bettina had told him back in the cabin, he knew this man was beholden only to himself. Erickson answered to no one else. "She loves you, you know."

John's disdain was obvious in his side glance.

"The trouble is," Stephen continued, "Bettina just never learned how to give love or receive it. I was never around enough to teach her how to show love. She lost her mother when she was a baby. She had no brothers or sisters." He paused, reflecting on his own past. "It's one of my greatest failings," he admitted weakly. "I had the love of a beautiful woman, and I loved her with all my heart. But—but I failed to teach my daughter how to have that same kind of love."

Erickson wasn't going to listen to this. He wasn't going to listen or feel anything. He was numb...numb...numb....

"She could do well with a man like you, one who can't be easily manipulated."

Erickson took a final drag on the cigarette and flicked it into the water below. "She needs a good spanking," he mumbled.

Bacheller chuckled at that and nodded. "Yes, she probably does. I never had the heart to do it when she was little." He shrugged. "So she always had her way. The world revolved around her."

Erickson was silent for a moment while he tried hard to keep his feelings buried beneath the heavy layer of ice that he had created to protect himself. He didn't want to feel anything for her. He didn't want to, but..."She was a lonely little girl, did you know that?"

230 *A Siren's Lure*

Bacheller glanced over at him in surprise. "You do care about her," he stated, a kind of low-keyed challenge in his voice. "And you're probably right. Again, my fault. But I would hate to see her go through the rest of her life being lonely."

Erickson knew that Bettina's father was staring at him, daring him to make a move of some sort. He turned toward the older man. "Listen, Mr. Bacheller, your daughter is beautiful...and..." He shook his head roughly in an effort to tighten his resolve. "But I'm out of the market. You and she can go tripping around the world together, spending all of your money, and she'll be as happy as a lark."

Stephen continued to stare hard at Erickson. "I don't think so. Not without you." He let go of the railing and walked over to the door, on his way back to the cabins below.

Erickson watched him go, then closed his eyes. He wasn't going to feel anything for her. He wasn't. No matter how good she looked...or felt...or...was....

He lit another cigarette and stared out over the cold, dark sea.

Chapter Seventeen

Early-afternoon sunlight splashed through the windows of the hotel room, scattering yellow bands across the bed and rug. The shutters were open to a view of the Roman Forum, lying below in all its neglected state. Huge columns tumbled over one another, and pieces of carved marble were strewn haphazardly about the ground. Up the street stood the magnificent structure of the Colosseum.

"What?" Bettina cried, standing in the middle of the room in a patch of sunshine that highlighted her blond hair. "Are you out of your mind?"

Erickson leaned back against the wall, his arms crossed, his eyes flicking over her with a kind of lazy disdain. "You set the plan in motion, Bettina. Why back out now?"

"John," she retorted impatiently, her nerves ragged from the cold treatment she had been receiving from him since last night, "Jerry McCluskey could put you behind bars for the rest of your life. All you have to do is take off from here. I'll tell him that we lost you. It's simple."

A half smile played around his mouth as he regarded her. Everything was so simple to her, black and white; nothing was complicated if one didn't make it that way. As much as he hated to admit it, he liked that about her. Liked it a lot. It was a freshness, a youthful quality, an optimism that he had lost at a very young age. With her, he almost felt as if he had never seen the grittier side of life. Almost.

"It's not simple, Bettina. I'm tired of running. So just call him up at his hotel and make arrangements to meet him."

She tilted her chin higher and squared off against him from across the room. "No."

He contemplated her combative posture. "If you don't, I will."

Bacheller was sitting on the edge of the bed, following the exchange as if he were at a tennis match.

"You're no help at all," Bettina snapped at her father, frustrated with her inability to talk some sense into that thick-headed mule of a man she loved.

Bacheller cleared his throat and stood up, reluctantly coming to his daughter's defense. He didn't really want to get involved in this situation any more than he already was. He liked Erickson and he loved Bettina. But a matchmaker he did not want to be. Whatever relationship they had was their own.

"I've known Jerry since he was a child," he offered hesitantly. "Maybe...maybe I could talk to him—convince him to stop looking for you."

Erickson stared at the older man and then chuckled dryly. "I didn't realize naiveté ran in the family. You of all people should understand there's no likelihood of something like that ever happening."

A Siren's Lure

Stephen Bacheller sat back on the edge of the bed, closed his mouth, and shrugged apologetically at his daughter.

"Now call, Bettina," Erickson ordered.

Bettina stared at him with a rapidly crumbling bravado. She tried to blink them away, but the tears kept filling her eyes anyway. Shaking her head slowly back and forth, she whispered painfully, "John, I can't make that call. I just can't."

"You can. All you have to do is pick up the phone and dial the number. Tell him to meet us on the Corso del Rinascimento. You got that? The Corso del Rinascimento. He'll know it. We've both...been there before."

"John, I..."

"Call, Bettina."

With one last pleading look at her father and then at John, she turned around, picked up the receiver and waited with closed eyes and a painful lump in her chest for the hotel operator to answer.

THEIR FEET TAPPED in odd, rhythmic patterns against the stone street as they walked. It was the only sound that any of them made. The air was warm, the sunlight angling from the western sky. The sounds and smells of the city were a blur as the three of them moved with a quiet intensity toward their destination.

The streets were dark and narrow, reflecting both the modern city that Rome now was and the ancient town that had not been built in a day. A glaring neon sign hung over a darkly carved baroque doorway; functionless ancient columns were propped up next to a glass-and-chrome bank entrance. But as they wound

234 *A Siren's Lure*

their way toward the Corso del Rinascimento, the older city took over. Pigeon droppings covered a small statue in the center of a fountain, the cobblestone street was pitted and uneven, and the sounds of the modern world faded farther away.

They were all silent as they walked, and Bettina felt as if she were going to jump out of her skin. An icy chill crept up her spine. Her heart was beating irregularly and much too fast. Several times she started to say something, to beg John to turn around and run while he still had the chance. But she had said it all before. And he had glazed over with an expression cut from marble, a facade that refused to listen to anyone other than himself. She kept telling herself that she couldn't let him do this; she loved him too much. But what could she do? There was certainly no way she could physically restrain him from doing what he wanted. She had no control over him.

They followed the edge of a building as it curved down another alleyway, dark and dank and smelling of spices. A woman was beating a rug on the balcony above them, and a scroungy dog sat in the middle of the road, scratching at fleas.

They rounded the last corner on Via Pie' di Marmo and stopped. Bettina knew that Erickson's heart had to be pounding as hard as hers was. A black BMW was parked at the end of the street, at the spot where the road curved up toward the Piazza della Minerva. Beyond the car was a sculptured stone elephant carrying a small Egyptian obelisk on its back. Bettina saw nothing but the shiny black car, only twenty feet away.

A Siren's Lure 235

All was silent, except for their breathing. She could hear Erickson's breath, now quick yet steady, beside her.

The car door opened and Jerry stepped out. Keeping the door open, he stood behind it with his arms resting on top of its frame.

A gun was in his right hand.

Bettina gasped, and her eyes jumped from Jerry to Erickson and back to Jerry again. Both men were watching each other as if they were the only two people who existed in the world.

"Jerry," she cried pitifully, "please don't do this! Please, for me..."

Concentrating solely on Erickson, Jerry spoke to him in an even voice. "It's been a long time, Erickson."

"Yes."

Bettina glanced at John's profile. It was as stiff as his response had been. The muscle in his jaw was the only thing that gave away his inner turmoil.

"Funny you should pick this spot to meet," Jerry said. "I remember it well."

"Yes, I thought you might."

Jerry wiped his forehead with the back of the hand that held the gun, then resumed pointing the pistol straight at Erickson. "What am I going to do with you?"

Erickson barely shrugged. "You're the man with all the power behind you."

"Yeah." Jerry nodded. "Breathing down my neck is more like it."

"You should have gone out into the field as I did."

236   *A Siren's Lure*

Jerry just chuckled. "I'm not a swamp rat, and you know it. I liked the easy life too much." Then he sighed heavily, a sound they all heard clearly in the quiet surrounding them. "I've got a job to do, you know. I've got to take you in."

Bettina felt as if something were about to implode within her; as if her body were crashing in on itself. Here she was, with the three most important men in her life—the man she loved, her father and her best friend—yet she was powerless to say or do anything. It was as if the ability to speak or cry out had been ripped from her mind and body. She wanted to cry; she wanted to cling to John; she wanted to throw something at Jerry. She wanted to run. But all she could do was listen helplessly to the man beside her speaking so calmly, so evenly, as if he were not crumbling inside.

"I can't live in a cage," he said quietly, but Jerry heard him well enough.

"We know you had nothing to do with Winston's dealings with the other side. We know you're clean on that score."

"Okay," Erickson conceded. "So I've been cleared of that. And I carried out my assignment—to steal those documents and destroy them. But what about the fact that I stole those jewels? What about the fact that I've been hiding out for five years? What does the brass think about all that?"

Jerry was too quiet, and Bettina squeezed her fists tightly at her side. Her father's hand reached over and unclenched her fist, wrapping the soft warmth of his fingers around her hand.

A Siren's Lure 237

"That's what I figured." Erickson nodded slowly, as if in response to the answer Jerry had not given. He shook his head. "Nope. I can't come in. So if you plan on using that thing, you might as well shoot now, because I won't go willingly back to the States with you."

Bettina's mouth dropped open. She was horrified that John could think Jerry would shoot him, that there was the possibility that Jerry—this man she had known since childhood—could actually shoot anyone. She was even more horrified when she saw Jerry shrug and heard him say, "If that's the way you want it...."

With a wild cry, she threw herself in front of Erickson. "Jerry! You can't do this! Please!"

Her father tried a more rational approach. "Jerry, I've known you since you were a little boy. You're not a killer. Let the man go."

Erickson grabbed Bettina's upper arm and set her aside, waiting calmly for Jerry to make the next move.

Seconds ticked by while Bettina held her breath and thought that her heart was not beating.

"Ah, hell!" Jerry muttered in frustration, tossing the gun onto the front seat of the car. He slowly withdrew a cigar from his pocket and flicked a lighter to it. A flame shot up and the end of the cigar glowed red.

Bettina stood with mouth agape, eyes wide and heart pounding like a jackhammer in her chest. Stephen was muttering, "What the hell?" to himself. But Erickson still hadn't moved a muscle. He was watching Jerry with a curious but tightly controlled expression.

Jerry held the cigar at arm's length. "Your favorite brand, as I recall."

238 *A Siren's Lure*

Bettina glanced at John and finally saw his shoulders sag in relief. Bewildered, she tagged along behind him as he walked toward the car and took the cigar from Jerry. He inhaled slowly, then released the smoke even more slowly.

The two men stared at each other, and finally Jerry shook his head in begrudging acceptance. "You son of a bitch." He moved away from the car door and they embraced, no longer two adversaries, now only two longtime friends. When they let go, Erickson was still watching him with a kind of speculative stare.

Jerry just shrugged. "You *would* have to pick this spot to meet, wouldn't you?"

Erickson's mouth curved up in a sly smile.

"I don't understand," Bettina said, her voice cracking as she gazed with wide eyes at Jerry. "I simply don't understand."

"I had it all worked out," he explained. "I had a job to do and...dammit, I was going to do it." He glanced at Erickson. "I really was."

"I know that," John said.

"But when I drove down this street..." He shook his head again. "You saved my life here once."

"We saved each other's," Erickson corrected.

Jerry chuckled softly. "I guess we did at that." He narrowed his eyes on his friend and muttered, "You *are* a son of a bitch." Then he turned to Stephen Bacheller. "And where the hell have *you* been, old man?"

Stephen laughed and vigorously shook Jerry's hand. They embraced, Bettina's father and the man who was the closest person to a son he had.

A Siren's Lure 239

While they laughed and embraced, Bettina touched Erickson's arm. He looked at her, but his expression remained inscrutable. There was so much she wanted to say to him, so many ways she wanted to tell him how much he meant to her and how bad she felt for deceiving him, but she couldn't speak for the lump in the back of her throat. Her eyes burned; tears spilled over and rolled down her cheeks.

Reaching out with the tip of his finger, Erickson gently wiped them away. But he didn't take her in his arms, and Bettina knew in that moment, with a realization that pierced her like a knife, that he might never take her in his arms again.

THE SUN WAS FADING rapidly in the west. A light breeze stirred up the fragrances of garlic and tomato in the air. The outdoor table was covered with a red-checkered cloth, the wine was a very dry Marino, and across the way was the Pantheon, one of Rome's best-preserved monuments and one of the world's greatest architectural achievements. In the center of the piazza, a fountain lay nearly burried beneath a cloud of pigeons. Two children and a dog splashed about in the water.

"I've been doing some research on your problem," Jerry informed Stephen.

"I have problems?" Stephen grinned, then took another drink of wine.

"Just a few, Dad," Bettina told him dryly. She glanced over at Erickson and smiled, wishing more than anything that she could have a few minutes alone with him—just him—to talk.

240 *A Siren's Lure*

Jerry leaned his elbows on the table and spoke across the table. "The U.S. government doesn't really care if you are alive or dead—or, for that matter, if you are Le Chat Noir. All they really wanted in the first place was the property to pay the back taxes with, and any other monies that might have been due. Now, I can get that figure if you're willing to pay it, and that will get them off your back and off Bettina's."

Stephen lifted his hands upward. "Anything."

Bettina turned to Jerry. "Is it really as simple as that?"

Jerry nodded. "The rest, as far as the U.S. is concerned, is Interpol's problem." He glanced at Bacheller and pointed a finger at him. "Unless you decide to set foot in the States, of course, and then it will be a whole new ball game."

Stephen took a hefty swig of the wine and poured himself another glass. "Believe me, I'm too old for any new games. I'll stick to the old ones, thank you."

Bettina's eyes lifted to the cool spray of water in the fountain and to the domed structure beyond, which was turning gray in the waning light. Groups of teenagers with green and orange streaks in their hair skated through the center of the piazza. But it was a furtive movement in the shadows that sent a chill slinking up her spine.

"John!" she whispered, reaching across the table to grasp his forearm. "It's him! I can't believe it!"

"Who?" Jerry and her father asked at the same time.

Erickson swung his head around and followed Bettina's gaze to the left side of the Pantheon. Alvin Bilgeworth, staggering along on crutches, was head-

A Siren's Lure   241

ing toward their table. Erickson looked back at Bettina with an expression that was clearly a mixture of annoyance and awe. "How the hell did he do that?"

"Who is it?" Stephen asked her.

"The man John threw off the train somewhere south of Salerno."

"Threw off the..."

Jerry laughed. "I see you haven't changed a bit, have you, Erickson?" He turned to Bettina. "So that's the insurance investigator you told me about?"

"Yes," she whispered fearfully as she watched Bilgeworth approaching. Her skin was crawling at the sight of him, but at least this time she was surrounded by three men who would protect her. Besides, he had never really been after her in the first place. He had always sought her father.

Bilgeworth swaggered—as best he could on crutches—up to their table and stopped. Erickson reached out to steady the bottle of Marino when Alvin's stomach almost knocked it over. His face was bruised, and a wide bandage stretched across the bridge of his nose. They all sat very still and stared at him as he fidgeted with his jacket, awkwardly extracting his gun and brandishing it in the air around them.

"Uh-oh," Jerry mimed in his Edward G. Robinson voice. "He's packing a rod."

"This is no joke," Alvin croaked. "I've got you all where I want you now."

A bored groan circled the table.

Jerry lazily pulled out his identification badge and tossed it on the tablecloth where Alvin could read it. "Now, put that damn thing away," he said. "Before

242 *A Siren's Lure*

you shoot something really important, like the wine bottle.''

Alvin glared at Jerry and swung his suspicious gaze around the table, but Bettina noticed that he quite conspicuously avoided any direct contact with Erickson's eyes. After several hostile seconds, he begrudgingly slipped the gun back into his jacket.

He concentrated on the man sitting beside Bettina. ''You're Stephen Bacheller, aren't you?'' he said gloatingly.

Stephen's eyes were twinkling with amusement as he glanced at Bettina. ''He's quick.''

''Dad,'' she murmured dryly, ''meet Alvin Bilgeworth, of Hopkins Mutual.''

Alvin was looking hard at Stephen. ''Le Chat Noir,'' he stated melodramatically.

Jerry laughed. ''That's real good, Alvin. Are you always that quick, or is this an exception?''

Alvin's gaze accidentally landed on Erickson, and he flinched under John's cold stare. He swallowed a few times and hurriedly shifted his eyes back to Stephen. ''I want the jewels, the ones you stole from Clarence Stanhope's wife.''

Bacheller looked back at him, not intimidated in the least. ''And if I don't give them to you?''

''Then I'll make it my job to hound you till one of us is dead.'' It had been such an effort for him to walk across the piazza that he was now panting as if his heart might give out at any second.

''That job may be a very short career,'' Stephen commented dryly, studying the pathetic slob standing there. ''And if I do give you what you want?''

A Siren's Lure 243

Alvin couldn't control himself. Unwittingly, his eyes traveled back to Erickson's taut face. Drops of sweat formed on his upper lip. "I'll—I'll go back to the States, and you..." His eyes flicked toward Erickson's face again. "You won't hear from me again."

"Sounds good to me," Stephen decided. He leaned over and picked up his cane from where it lay on the ground beside his chair. Pausing for only a second, he handed the cane over to Alvin.

"What the hell is this?" the insurance investigator grumbled.

"This, my dear man, is what you are looking for." Alvin was regarding the cane suspiciously, so Stephen added, "Go ahead, unscrew the handle."

Bilgeworth carefully did what he was told, then tipped the cane over. From inside the hollow shaft, the jewels poured into his fat hand. Glancing around frantically to see if anyone had noticed, he quickly stuffed some of the jewels into his pockets and crammed the rest back down into the cane. He then screwed the lid back on.

Jerry sat back in his chair and lifted his wineglass. "Don't forget I'm a witness to this, Alvin, old boy...just in case you had any ideas of...well, you know, heading for Easy Street with the jewels."

Alvin glared at Jerry, then adjusted the cane under his arm. He turned and started to hobble off on his crutches.

"Bilgeworth." The one word was uttered low between clenched teeth, but the sound stopped him dead in his tracks. He turned around very slowly, his eyes bulging with remembered fear. Sweat broke out anew on his lip and forehead while he waited for Erickson

244   *A Siren's Lure*

to speak. "If I ever—*ever*—catch you near this man or this woman again, I'll kill you. Is that clear?"

Not doubting for a minute that Erickson would indeed kill him, Alvin swallowed hard and struggled to wipe the thick bank of sweat off his forehead. He turned around without saying a word and staggered away.

It was very quiet at the table after he had left. No one seemed inclined to speak. Bettina was watching Erickson. Anger still smoldered deep within him. It was in his eyes and in the line of his jaw.

"So," Stephen finally said, clearing his throat. "Two down, one to go. That takes care of that dogged insurance investigator and the IRS. All that's left is Interpol."

Jerry shrugged. "Can't help you there, old man."

"You have done enough," Stephen said, laying a hand on his arm. "You have given my daughter back to me. That is worth everything."

Bettina smiled and reached for his hand.

"And now," her father said quietly, "now I must go."

"Go!" she cried, nearly upsetting her glass as she pulled her hand back. "Why? Go where?"

He reached out and gently touched her face. "Interpol has not given up on Le Chat Noir, Bettina. So I must not stay still for very long. A glass of wine here, a warm summer evening with a beautiful woman there...Moments, Bettina. That is my life now."

Her eyes began to fill yet again with tears as she stared at him, uncomprehending. "But—but we just got here. You've had a very harrowing experience...."

A Siren's Lure   245

"I like my life, Bettina. I do not want to sit in a rocking chair somewhere and reminisce about the old days. That is not for me."

"But what will you do? Where will you go?" she whispered tearfully.

He shrugged. "I do not know. But I will tell you this, my darling daughter.... I will not disappear from your life the way I did seven years ago. That was a mistake. And—and now that we've found each other again, I don't want to lose you. We will find ways to see each other. Often. I promise you that."

He leaned over and kissed her tear-streaked cheek. Then, sighing, he stood up and looked at Erickson. "What I said to you on the deck of the ship...Sometimes it is easier, as I said—but it is always more lonely."

They regarded each other for a long moment, during which a new level of understanding passed between them.

"I owe you my life," Stephen continued. "Someday, I hope I can repay you."

Erickson held out his hand and clasped Stephen's. "Take care of yourself."

"Yes, I will try."

Bettina was sobbing freely as she stumbled to her feet and reached out for him. "Daddy, please don't go!" she cried, knowing that no matter what she said, he would go anyway. "I love you...."

She fell into his arms and held him as if she would never let go. She wanted to believe that she would see him again. She wanted to believe it with all her heart. But she knew with a certainty that burned like fire inside her that someday he would be caught or even

246 *A Siren's Lure*

killed. *Will I ever see you again, Daddy,* she cried to herself. *Will you ever hold me in your arms again?*

She stepped back and sniffled, wiping her cheeks with her fingers. She had to let him go. This was his life. She lifted her chin and, through a veil of tears, saw him smile. Then he turned and walked away, across the Piazza della Rotonda and down the Via dei Pastini. After he had rounded the corner, he disappeared.

Bettina stood there for a long time, staring blankly in the direction her father had taken. She wanted to believe that the pain of losing him was now over. But she knew it had only just begun.

From the periphery of her eyes, she saw that Erickson was standing beside the table, his jacket flipped over one shoulder and held by the crook of his finger. Her breath stopped as she pivoted slowly and stared at him.

"I, too, have to go," he said, very quietly but with a tone of finality that left no room for arguments or pleas.

Her heart, as well as her breathing, seemed to have stopped. She couldn't get her lungs going again. Something was stuck painfully in her chest. He was leaving her. *Leaving her.* He was really going to go. She would never see him again. Never. Upton John Erickson would make certain that he left no traces.

She watched in a painful daze as he shook hands with Jerry. "What will you tell the agency?" he asked.

Jerry studied his friend for a long time. "That you're dead. I was the only one who kept on looking for you. I was the only one who knew where you might be."

A Siren's Lure 247

Erickson nodded slowly, and the gruffness in his voice revealed the emotion that was churning inside him at that moment. "Thanks, McCluskey."

Jerry clasped his hand tightly, then released him and sat back down at the table.

Erickson stood still for a hesitant moment, wondering what was the best way to handle this. He hadn't looked at Bettina yet and he didn't think he should. If he didn't turn around and look at her, he'd be okay. If he didn't have to see those green eyes watching him, or that pale face he wanted to touch, or that golden hair he could feel even now between his fingers...If he didn't look, he could just walk away. It would be over. Fast and painless.

He took a deep breath and pivoted away from the table.

Bettina was paralyzed with a fear she had never known before. How could she just let him walk away? She loved him! No matter what his name was, no matter what color his hair was or his eyes were, it was the man underneath the protective facade whom she loved.

"John?" she called. He wasn't going to turn around. He wasn't even going to look at her....

The blood was pounding in her temples; her eyes burned; her throat felt scratchy and dry. She could hear laughter in the piazza and the clink of glasses in gay toasts. The air was heavy with the smell of spices and cool with the dying day. Her skin prickled along her arms. Sharp fingers inched their way up her spine. Something clutched her stomach and wouldn't let go. Pain. Fear. A terrible loneliness. The loneliness had always been there, but this time it hurt much worse. And she wouldn't let it happen.

She couldn't.

Her mother had left her when she was two; her father had just walked out of her life for the second time. And now—now the only man she had ever wanted to spend her life with was leaving her, taking her lifeblood with him as he went. He was leaving her with nothing more substantial than a memory of him.

Turn around, damn you! Turn around! "John!"

At the gut-wrenching sound of his name as it tore from her throat, he automatically turned around.

It was a grave mistake.

That one tactical error was going to cost him everything—his heart, his soul, his life.

How could he even think of walking away from her now? When there was that much pain in her voice and agony in her eyes, how could he do it? He loved her. He had never loved a woman before in his life. Not like this. Not this much. No matter what she had done to trick him, he knew she had paid enough with her own guilt. In the past twenty-four hours, he had tried to believe that she was only deceitful and cunning, but he knew she was not. She was just...Bettina.

She walked over to him and lifted her face to meet those moist, earth-colored eyes. And she saw it all there, the love that neither of them had verbalized, but that now consumed their hearts and minds and bodies. And she knew that if he left her, he would be torn apart as much as she would be.

"You can't walk away from me," she whispered. "You can't. I'll follow you. I'd find you. No matter where you went."

A Siren's Lure 249

He clasped the back of her neck fiercely, pulling her face against his chest. With eyes closed, he pressed his face into the fragrant field of her hair. "Even if I went to Madagascar?" he murmured low against her scalp.

"Yes. Even if you went all the way to the ends of the earth."

He cupped her face between his hands and looked down at her, his eyes full of all the things that he wanted to say. "You're right, you know. I can't walk away from you." He shook his head roughly. "But...I should."

"No, you shouldn't. We belong together. We're all alone in the world, you and I. We have to take care of each other."

He frowned into her green eyes and ran his thumbs over her tears. "It won't be easy, Bettina. I want you to understand that."

She smiled weakly. "I've had easy, John. All my life. I don't want that anymore. I want love instead. I want to be a part of your life."

Lowering his head, he fastened his mouth possessively over hers and formed the words against her lips— the words she had waited all her life to hear. "I love you. I need you so much."

She reached up and stroked the hard plane of his jaw. "I love you, too. And I want to be with you wherever you are."

With his arms wrapped around her, still holding her close, Erickson glanced over her head toward the café table. Jerry was staring down into his wineglass, a glum expression on his face. "McCluskey is...more than just a friend, isn't he?"

250 *A Siren's Lure*

Bettina sighed against the front of his shirt. "Only from his viewpoint, John. He has always been a dear friend to me, but—but only that."

"How is he going to take this—us?"

"Graciously," she said. "He's a man with a lot of class."

Erickson nodded. "Yeah, he is that. Well, maybe we'd better go over and do some explaining."

They walked back to the table, but when Bettina saw the expression on Jerry's face, she said, "I don't think an explanation is necessary. I think it's quite clear."

Jerry was fingering his glass and looking up at his two best friends. He was trying to pull his thoughts and his emotions together. *Erickson is once again going to disappear into the sunset. And Bettina...well, I've lost her for sure now. Whatever chance I might have had to make her mine is definitely gone.* He pushed his chair back and stood up, expelling a fatalistic sigh. You win some, you lose some. That's just the way it is.

"I told you I'd let the agency know that you were dead, Erickson. I—I'm doing it as much for Bettina as for you. But if you ever do anything—anything at all—to hurt her...I'll reopen the case."

Erickson nodded slowly; he understood full well that Jerry would follow through with the threat where Bettina was concerned.

"Now, I've got the car," Jerry said, pointing up the street. "The government is paying for it and...seems a shame to see it go to waste. So how about a ride?"

Erickson put his arm around Bettina. "Sure, why not?"

A Siren's Lure 251

"Okay." Jerry nodded, quietly accepting the reality of his own loss. "So where do you want to go?"

They started walking toward the BMW. Bettina glanced at John and then grinned. Her smile grew positively devilish. "You know, I could use a bit of Shangri-la right now."

Erickson chuckled. "He did ask where we want to go, didn't he?"

Bettina caught Jerry's bewildered gaze. He was trying without much success to follow their cryptic conversation. "He did at that," she agreed.

They reached the car, and Jerry opened the back door for them. "I'll play chauffeur."

"After you." Erickson smiled at Bettina. She climbed into the backseat and he followed her in.

Jerry settled himself behind the wheel and glanced in the rearview mirror. "So..." he said again, "where do you two want to go?"

"You mean anywhere?" Erickson asked.

"Sure," Jerry insisted, "anywhere."

Erickson pulled the door of the BMW shut and wrapped a strong arm around Bettina's shoulder. She snuggled deep into the side of his body. Maybe sometime they would go back to Capri, to that secluded white house on the jagged cliff, to the isolated café on Punta Azzurra where it all began, to the flowers and the fragrant scent of oranges and lemons, to the pine breezes and the grottoes and the deep blue sea. But for now, they would go as far away as possible, to the end of the earth to find a bit of Shangri-la....

To find each other.

"Jerry," she said, smiling sweetly at his reflection in the mirror. "We have a little place in mind...."

You're invited to accept 4 books and a surprise gift ***Free!***

Acceptance Card

Mail to: Harlequin Reader Service®

In the U.S.
2504 West Southern Ave.
Tempe, AZ 85282

In Canada
P.O. Box 2800, Postal Station A
5170 Yonge Street
Willowdale, Ontario M2N 6J3

YES! Please send me 4 free Harlequin Temptation® novels and my free surprise gift. Then send me 4 brand new novels every month as they come off the presses. Bill me at the low price of $1.99 each ($1.95 in Canada)—a 13% saving off the retail price. There are no shipping, handling or other hidden costs. There is no minimum number of books I must purchase. I can always return a shipment and cancel at any time. Even if I never buy another book from Harlequin, the 4 free novels and the surprise gift are mine to keep forever.

142 BPX-BPGE

Name _____ (PLEASE PRINT)

Address _____ Apt. No. _____

City _____ State/Prov. _____ Zip/Postal Code _____

This offer is limited to one order per household and not valid to present subscribers. Price is subject to change.

ACHT-SUB-1

Author JOCELYN HALEY,
also known by her fans as SANDRA FIELD and JAN MACLEAN, now presents her eighteenth compelling novel.

DREAM OF DARKNESS

With the help of the enigmatic Bryce Sanderson, Kate MacIntyre begins her search for the meaning behind the nightmare that has haunted her since childhood.

Together they will unlock the past and forge a future.

Available in NOVEMBER or reserve your copy for September shipping by sending your name, address and zip or postal code, along with a check or money order for $4.70 (includes 75¢ for postage and handling) payable to Worldwide Library Reader Service to:

Worldwide Library Reader Service

In the U.S.:
Box 52040,
Phoenix, Arizona
85072-2040

In Canada:
5170 Yonge St., P.O. Box 2800
Postal Station A,
Willowdale, Ontario M2N 6J3

She fought for a bold future until she could no longer ignore the...

ECHO OF THUNDER

MAURA SEGER

Author of **Eye of the Storm**

ECHO OF THUNDER is the love story of James Callahan and Alexis Brockton, who forge a union that must withstand the pressures of their own desires and the challenge of building a new television empire.

Author Maura Seger's writing has been described by *Romantic Times* as having a "superb blend of historical perspective, exciting romance and a deep and abiding passion for the human soul."

Available in SEPTEMBER or reserve your copy for August shipping by sending your name, address and zip or postal code, along with a cheque or money order for—$4.70 (includes 75¢ for postage and handling) payable to Worldwide Library Reader Service to:

Worldwide Library Reader Service

In the U.S.:
Box 52040,
Phoenix, Arizona,
85072-2040

In Canada:
5170 Yonge Street, P.O. Box 2800,
Postal Station A,
Willowdale, Ontario, M2N 6J3

You're invited to accept 4 books and a surprise gift Free!

Acceptance Card

Mail to: Harlequin Reader Service®

In the U.S.
2504 West Southern Ave.
Tempe, AZ 85282

In Canada
P.O. Box 2800, Postal Station A
5170 Yonge Street
Willowdale, Ontario M2N 6J3

YES! Please send me 4 free Harlequin Superromance® novels and my free surprise gift. Then send me 4 brand new novels every month as they come off the presses. Bill me at the low price of $2.50 each—a 10% saving off the retail price. There are no shipping, handling or other hidden costs. There is no minimum number of books I must purchase. I can always return a shipment and cancel at any time. Even if I never buy another book from Harlequin, the 4 free novels and the surprise gift are mine to keep forever.

134 BPS-BPGE

Name _____ (PLEASE PRINT)

Address _____ Apt. No.

City _____ State/Prov. _____ Zip/Postal Code

This offer is limited to one order per household and not valid to present subscribers. Price is subject to change.

ACSR-SUB-1

Just what the woman on the go needs!

BOOKMATE

The perfect "mate" for all Harlequin paperbacks!

Holds paperbacks open for hands-free reading!

- TRAVELING
- VACATIONING
- AT WORK • IN BED
- COOKING • EATING
- STUDYING

Perfect size for all standard paperbacks, this wonderful invention makes reading a pure pleasure! Ingenious design holds paperback books OPEN and FLAT so even wind can't ruffle pages—leaves your hands free to do other things. Reinforced, wipe-clean vinyl-covered holder flexes to let you turn pages without undoing the strap...supports paperbacks so well, they have the strength of hardcovers!

Snaps closed for easy carrying.

Available now. Send your name, address, and zip or postal code, along with a check or money order for just $4.99 + .75¢ for postage & handling (for a total of $5.74) payable to Harlequin Reader Service to:

Harlequin Reader Service

In the U.S.A.
2504 West Southern Ave.
Tempe, AZ 85282

In Canada
P.O. Box 2800, Postal Station A
5170 Yonge Street,
Willowdale, Ont. M2N 5T5